GROUP

by Heather E. Robyn

For Maddy and Deegan,

Thank you.

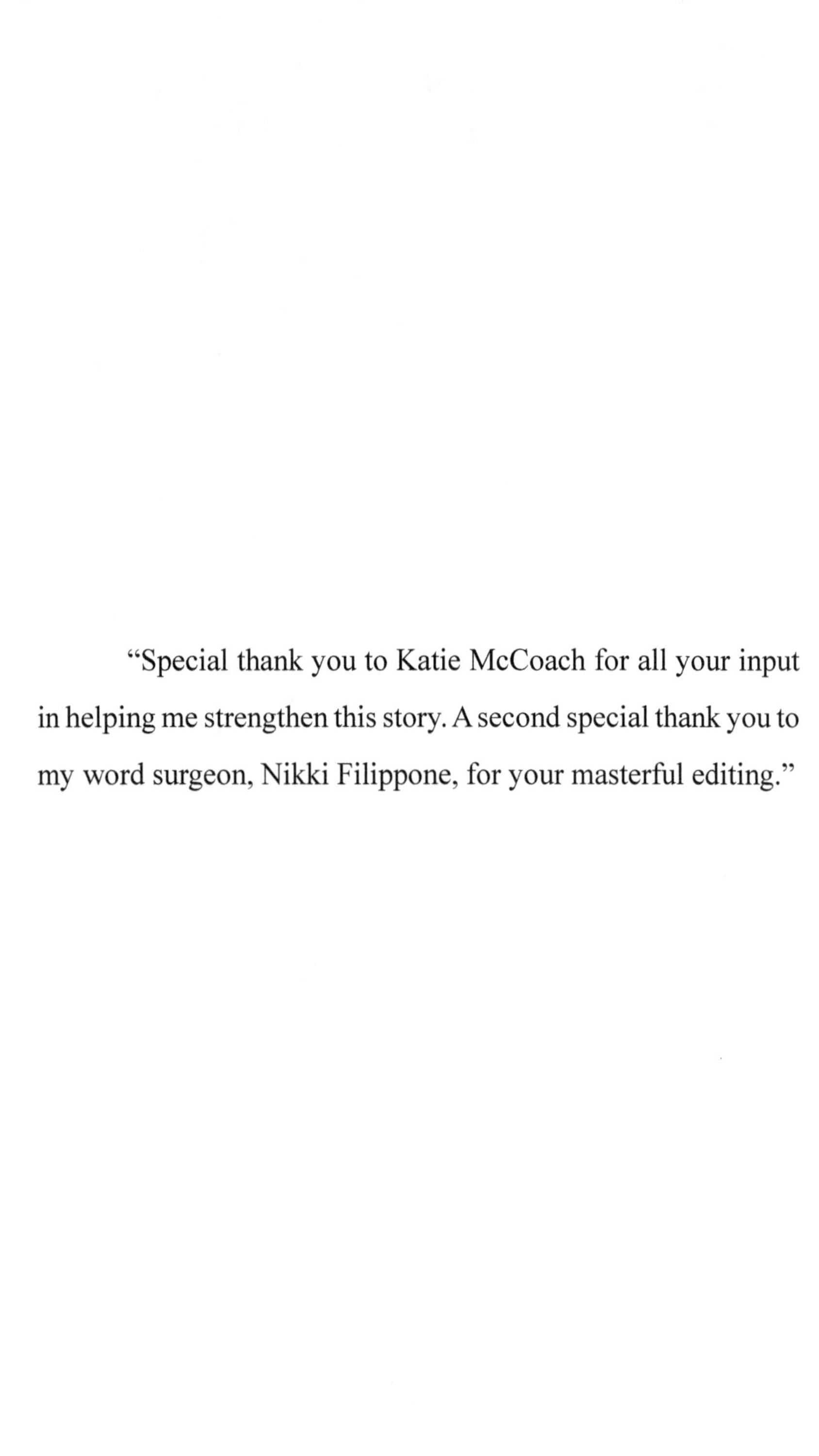

"Special thank you to Katie McCoach for all your input in helping me strengthen this story. A second special thank you to my word surgeon, Nikki Filippone, for your masterful editing."

ONE

"GROUP" the sign read. The inviting font of Cooper Sans, as if enticing one to join a party, might as well have been flashing in neon lights, too bright to ignore. Jade had walked by the sign every day since her arrival, and, every day, it felt like a gut punch telling her, "Guess what, kid, you're dead." For a second, Jade tried calculating how long she had been there. She knew she woke up every day. She knew she traveled the corridor and gave the sign a side-eye as she passed. But the days were a blur. As she tried to calculate the number of days she'd been there, she fidgeted with the collar of her white cotton-blend polo.

This shirt is so uncomfortable.

White was never her favorite color to wear. She remembered how it was especially susceptible to filth when she demolished her opponents countless times on the lacrosse field.

Why her coach chose white jerseys, she will never understand.

Jade made her daily journey through the corridor of the newly "welcomed" housing complex. It reminded her of the dorms at Boston University when she toured the previous summer. Her dwelling consisted of a single ten-by-ten-foot room with a desk, bookshelf, and twin bed.

Today, she stopped at the doors. Stopped and stared. Stood there with her wavy, copper, shoulder-length hair, olive skin, and green eyes that were stuck in a trance by the sign. Named for her green eyes like the jade stone, which means good luck, Jade didn't feel very lucky being there at only seventeen. A new Group session began today, but like every day before, Jade questioned her ability to step into the room rather than running down the hall and outside of whatever this place is called.

"Why do you always wait so long to make decisions?" Pearl whispered in Jade's mind. Pearl played the role of Jade's conscience growing up, imparting words of wisdom and caution on her to keep her on track whenever rambunctiousness kicked in.

I could use some wisdom right now, Pearl. There's such a gap in my heart. Please guide me.

"Thinking about giving it a try today, child?" a voice introjected from behind.

Jade rolled her eyes and said nothing. She had failed

to notice Miss Adelaide standing there, observing her like a zoologist observes animal behavior. It reminded her of when she volunteered at the local zoo in middle school.

Adelaide was Jade's transition caseworker, tasked with ensuring that Jade progressed through the program. Adelaide spoke softly and smiled frequently, and her cocoa eyes exuded friendliness. Murdered in her college dorm room fall semester of her junior year in 1973, Adelaide's death had rocked the community, and the Media had dubbed her the "roommate who suffered someone else's fate." Her roommate's ex-boyfriend had sought revenge for a nasty break up and Adelaide had fallen into a wrong place, wrong time scenario.

"Is there anything I can do to help?"

"Some color in my room would be fabulous. The whole grayscale theme is so tired. Even the desk and bed frame are gray. The only color that pops in it is my hair."

"The color scheme is meant to keep you calm."

"Blue keeps me calm. So does green. Are all the rooms this way?"

"Unfortunately, yes. We like to keep a neutral base."

"What a shame."

Adelaide shook her head and snickered. "On a serious note. Are you going to give Group a try today?"

Her words burned Jade's brain. *Pushy. So damn pushy.*

"It's been too long. You're not leaving me with many case notes on your progress."

Why does she even need to keep case notes? Why is protocol implemented in the first place? What a confusing place. It's delightful yet cold. Somber, but friendly. No real title holds the name here.

Jade's eyes zig-zagged as she exhaled.

"My arrival here was swift and uneventful. I sat in a waiting room that replicated a physician's office. But I was alone in that room. Blinding white and sterile looking as though a wave of bleach engulfed the room, sanitizing everything in its path. It screamed, "don't touch," but I didn't want to touch, I wanted to understand. The couch cushions were plush, but to me, they felt like straw poking at my back with uneasy tension, welcoming me to this new and uncomfortable place. Then I met you. You explained how to proceed to the next level and provided daily guidance and check-ins. I know Group is the first goal I have to accomplish. I just don't feel *there* yet."

"What's holding you back?"

"Nothing. I don't feel like it today."

"A bit feisty with that response, aren't we?"

"I'm sorry, I didn't mean to snap," Jade replied. "Just thinking a lot about Pearl today. Wondering if she's thinking of me. Every day I pass this room with no desire to go inside."

"What's stopping you? You've been standing here for almost fifteen minutes. Group already started, child."

What's stopping me?

"Nothing. Nothing is stopping me."

Jade glanced over to Adelaide, catching the enormous grin stretched across her face.

"Why are you smiling?"

"Because you are ready."

Jade focused back on the sign.

GROUP.

What's stopping me? I don't know. I'll never know unless I go. Fine. I'll go.

She took a step forward, then another, until she stood in an unfamiliar room filled with a familiar scent.

Vanilla cookies. Just like grandma's.

In the room sat seven teens and a facilitator, Chase. Jade had seen Chase several times during her journeys down the corridor and in the garden. He stood tall with a lanky build and long delicate fingers. He was exceptionally nice and good-hearted. She continued advancing toward the group. *Dang, these people are so young. How did they die? Do they feel as lost as I do right now?*

"What a wonderful surprise to see you here, Jade," Chase announced. His head tilted to the side, a smirk painted on his face.

"Hello everyone," Jade said as she raised her left hand in slow motion, stopping it at her waist, then flailing out her fingers and flapping them. The group stared at her for a second. Stared. *How awkward.*

"Why don't you join us? We have an open seat right here for you. Ezekiel, can you please bring a chair up for Jade?"

"Sure, no problem," Ezekiel responded as he stood up and turned toward Jade. His crystal blue eyes immediately caught her attention. She gazed fixedly at them as he approached. "Hello. I'm Ezekiel. My friends call me Zeek."

"Hi Jade," escaped her lips before she could stop herself. Her hand was frozen at the hip, failing to extend to meet his handshake. Ezekiel tilted his head to the side, then retracted his hand and proceeded past Jade, picking up the spare chair sitting by the door.

Way to go, idiot.

"Jade, it's nice to meet you. You can sit next to me if you want," Ezekiel said, knocking her tricep with his elbow as he passed her and situated the chairs in the circle.

Be cool, girl, be cool.

Jade cleared her throat and replied, "Sure. Thanks. Nice to meet you too."

"Let's continue, shall we?" Chase intruded. "Since today

is the first day of the new group and we were all sharing how we arrived here, let's pick up where we left off."

A few members were left to share their stories. Tracy, from Detroit, was a bystander who was shot during a gang fight on her way home from volleyball practice. As an only child, her mother raised her alone after her father passed away. She was fourteen when she died. Allister, from Connecticut, lost his battle with leukemia two weeks after high school graduation at the age of eighteen. He received an academic scholarship to Harvard and expressed his disappointment in not pursuing his law degree. Cassandra (Cass for short) died in a freak accident during a family trip. She slipped on a rock and fell off the side of a cliff while taking photos with her family. Her father tried pulling her up, but she slipped from his grip and fell to her death. She was fifteen.

Ezekiel already shared his story, so Jade missed the opportunity to hear it.

Now I regret staring at the sign outside for so long. What happened to him? What was he like in school? Where did he live? How old is he?

Chase turned his attention to Jade and asked, "Jade, would you like to share your story?"

She sat, staring into an oblivion on the floor when it finally came to her. She lifted her head up with a blank expression and looked at each member of the group one by one—each staring back at her with anticipation. Her neck tingled as perspiration built on her forehead. Jade looked at Chase as numbness enveloped her mind. She took a deep breath and, in a cracked voice, rattled out, "I…I…I don't know how I died."

TWO

Why is he bothering me again? I wish he would go away.

Please go away, Jamie.

The hallway light crept into the pitch-black bedroom as Jamie opened Pearl's door and peeked in.

"Pearl," he whispered.

Nothing.

"Pearl."

Nothing.

"Hey, get up!" he demanded as he flicked on the light and stepped back—her catatonic state not averted. No sound. Sleeping. Jamie retreated from the safety of the door jam and sat down on Pearl's bed, his leg touching her knee.

"You can't keep doing this."

Pearl said nothing.

"You're not the only one who misses her. We all do; me, mom, dad, Andrew. We all miss her, but we are trying to recover, and I think it is time you do the same. You've been like this for too long."

Silence filled the air, and a rebuttal never surfaced.

"You know what, I'm leaving in the next few weeks to start workouts for next season, and I don't want to leave knowing you are still in this shape."

A shoulder twitched.

Pearl's eyelids fluttered as they gradually embraced the light. Her pupils struggled to focus as intentional irritation streamed across her face.

"Not today."

"Today."

"Tomorrow."

"Today."

"Why do I have to go today? Why can't I go when I am ready?"

"Because if you don't go today, you won't go tomorrow or the next day, and I'm done seeing you like this. It's been months. I am attending Group today. You should come with me. It will help you to start talking about this. Group starts in an hour and a half. You may want to hurry and get yourself together."

He has no idea what it's like.

Pearl nodded.

"Good, meet me downstairs at 9:30. I'll drive. Love ya, kid."

Shy from looking like a tinman without oil, Pearl rose from her bed and headed to the bathroom. Her movements were rigid, and her pace mirrored a geriatric patient, but she made way to her destination. She stood in the bathroom, gazing at the image that stared back; her blurred vision not recognizing the gangly, skeletal girl staring back at her with matted black hair and powder white skin. She looked at her brush, sitting lonely on the counter.

I'm sure you miss me, don't you?

Energy failed her again today, so the brush remained where it sat. She remembered for a second how her past self enjoyed the morning beauty routine of hair and makeup, but those days had long since passed. She exhaled sharply as her examination continued.

It's going to take forever to get these knots out. Bun day it is.

Her gray sweater hung off her right shoulder, tattered with the stench of daily wear, "Boston University" peeking through the wrinkles across the chest. Her black leggings dangled on her knees like oversized sweatpants. She slipped her maroon boots on, one at a time. *At least my feet still fit into something.*

……

The sun burned Pearl's skin as Jamie rolled the passenger window down. Her eyes ping-ponged from side to side, following the trees as they zoomed past the car window, the air danced on her face, reminding her of junior prom. Her eyes now fixed as she stared through the rays produced by the leaves in the sky. The memory of hanging out in the limo sunroof pained her heart as she remembered that senior prom wouldn't happen this year. Her eyelids closed and produced darkness.

"I love the feeling of air on my face," Pearl said.

"I can see why dogs enjoy this," Jade said.

"You're so silly."

"Right back atcha, girl."

"Could this night get any better?"

"I don't know, Junior Princess. Could it?"

Jade flicked Pearl's crown with her index finger.

"Look at the bank clock; it's 11:11. Make a wish."

Both girls squinted their eyes. Jade opened her right eye and smiled at Pearl as she stood there in deep focus, making her wish.

"Rabbit punch!"

"Ouch, Jade! Why do you always have to punch me in the arm like that?"

"Because it's fun, and I know you enjoy it."

"Oh, you're such a punk. Give me a squeeze, sis."

"What was that?" Jamie asked.

"What was what?" Pearl said, reality welcoming her back as she massaged her shoulder.

"You said to make a wish. A wish for what?"

"Oh, nothing."

"Hmm."

……

"Welcome, everyone. Looks like we have a new member today. Would you like to introduce yourself?" Albert asked.

Pearl's eyes glazed over as she made eye contact. "You have green eyes," she said before she could stop herself. "My sister, Jade, has… had green eyes."

"Is this why you are here? Because of Jade?"

Why would he ask me that?

"Okay, let's start with a name, what do you say? I am Albert. What is your name?"

"Shouldn't you know it? My brother has been coming here, and I am sure he has spoken about me."

Albert sat silent, staring at Pearl.

"Pearl."

"Pearl, it is great to meet you. Would you be comfortable if we started Group right now? You are more than welcome to listen in today. Nobody here is forced to participate if they do not feel comfortable. Okay?"

I don't even want to be here.

Pearl nodded in compliance.

Albert continued with Group. A dozen individuals introduced themselves to Pearl and provided condolences.

Condolences mean nothing to me. I needed to hear her voice, her laugh, her sigh. I need to feel her rabbit punch to my shoulder every time she caught the clock at 11:11. I wish you were here right now, Jade. But you're not and never will be. Why am I even here? It'll never help. If they could all shut up and stop giving condolences, that would be great. Condolences got me here in the first place.

Her head slumped as she listened to stories of accidents, cancer, disease, and a robbery gone wrong.

I just want to scream. Do they know this won't help? Why are they all being so naïve?

Sandy began sharing about her husband of thirty-five years who recently died of prostate cancer when Pearl lifted her head and interrupted in a cracked tone. "I killed my sister."

Silence.

……

"Why would you say that?" Jamie shouted to Pearl as they entered the front door.

Go to hell, Jamie.

"What happened?" Marlene questioned.

"Pearl told the group she killed Jade."

"She said what?"

"She interrupted another group member in the middle of an emotional share about her husband and literally said, 'I killed my sister.' Why can't she get on the wagon like the rest of us and start processing so she can move on?"

"Jamie, she was there when Jade died. She is dealing with some level of survivor's guilt over what happened. We need to be patient with her and let her heal in her own time."

"This is bullshit,"

"Language, mister. You may be in college, but in this house, you will be respectful. Clear?"

"Yes, Ma'am. I don't understand, Mom. You would think Pearl would know that Jade wouldn't want this."

"Oh, sweetie, Pearl will recover in her own time. We need to be patient."

Jamie threw his hands in the air and exhaled as he marched to the couch to watch Sports Avenue. Marlene did an about-face, making her way to the kitchen window, reminding herself to breathe as she closed her eyes to concentrate. Tracking her breath in and out until she became calm, she opened her eyes to focus on the plethora of roses guarding the front ledge of the kitchen window. A tear escaped her eye as she remembered the day Jade stood in front of those roses posing for pre-prom pictures. Jade stood in her cobalt blue, form-fitting, high slit gown, smiling with her friend, Josh. Jade had spent months trying to convince her mother of the appropriateness of wearing a dress that showed nearly her entire back and a third of her cleavage. Initially, Marlene had fought the idea, but looking back, she was glad she let Jade wear the dress.

At least she was happy

Marlene always butted heads with Jade about strictness. Jade debated relentlessly with her mother about clothes, music—even what classes she should take for her electives. Marlene inhaled and repeated her reminder, *At least she was happy*. The double-ping text notification sound jolted Marlene from her memory visit.

ANDY: What time is dinner, Mom?

MOM: 7

ANDY: Sweet. Boys and I are heading to the lake

for a bit. See you tonight. Love ya. L8S.

MOM: ok. xoxo

She trucked up the stairs to her bedroom to steal a short nap before dinner, when she stopped at Pearl and Jade's bedroom. Marlene leaned on the door, anticipating the sound of sobbing emanating from the other side of the wooden slate separating her from her daughter, but she heard nothing. As she reached for the door handle, she stopped herself mid-grip and backed away from the door with her left palm still firmly placed on it, ready to turn it if Pearl requested her presence. She moved her index finger slightly to the left to reveal a small letter J carved into the door. Jade's preteen handy work. Emotionally spent from the endless series of memories, Marlene dropped her hand from the door and hastily made her way to her bedroom. She threw herself on the bed, sobbing until she could no longer cry, and fell asleep.

......

Pearl didn't come down for dinner. When she finally came to, she rolled over to see how much time had passed. Pearl sat up when she observed that the clock read 11:11. She rubbed her shoulder, lost in her memory of the time Jade caught her off-guard in tenth grade.

"Sucker punch!" Jade yelled as she jumped from the elevated wall in the campus quad, knocking Pearl square in her right deltoid. "It's 11:11 Pearl, make a wish."

"Damn it, Jade. You made me drop my soda." Pearl said as she leaned down to pick up the plastic bottle now solid with pressure, ready to explode.

"It will survive," Jade said. "Just make the wish."

Pearl backhanded Jade. "Ugh, fine." She squinted her

eyes for a few seconds to make her wish. Jade flicked her on the nose, causing Pearl's eyes to abruptly open and wince at Jade before giggling at her sister's silly action. Jade smiled back at her sister as the two continued to the lunch line to purchase their favorite snack… drumsticks.

In the darkness, Pearl whispered to herself, "Make a wish, Pearl." She stood up and made her way to the bedroom door. She swung the door open and fumbled her spider-like figure down the steps into the kitchen to make an ice cream sundae with chocolate ice cream, fudge, caramel, whipped cream… and two spoons.

THREE

Jade had been unsuccessful in solving the mystery of why she died.

Why am I still in Group? Because I can't seem to concentrate at all on my progress?

Members came and went. Savannah stayed for only one session; Desmond stayed for three. Most attended just two sessions. Jade tracked comings and goings on the whiteboard in her room. Most didn't stay as long as she had, except Ezekiel. Jerome sat in the circle as one of the newest members and told his story to a highly attentive audience. The participants discussed how dying felt.

Jerome looked down as he began to speak. "It didn't feel how I imagined. I hung there waiting, which seemed like forever. It was like time stood still so I could absorb my choices—my conscience telling me, 'This is what you get for killing yourself kid.' I don't remember a lot of pain, just that it just took forever. When I began fading, a small part of me kept thinking that maybe it wasn't the best idea, but I didn't try to stop. People can talk about how suicide is not the solution, but when you are going through it, it's not suicide to you; it's a solution to end the pain."

In a previous session, he had shared that he grew up in a small town in Texas. His voice had a soft cowboy drawl to it when he spoke, which reminded Jade of the Western movies she watched as a child. He grew up on a dairy farm and helped his father with daily chores during the summer months.

"I began thinking about other people," Jerome continued. "Thinking about how sad mom would be, how mad dad would be, what the kids at school would think about me... The hardest person to think about was my little sister. She was only seven. How would she understand this, you know? Her brother sent himself to heaven because he was picked on?"

How awful.

"What if *she* found me? Then I would have scarred her for life. But even this didn't give me the energy to try and stop. I feel like I let her down because she looked up to me, and now I won't be there. To think I did this while they were all downstairs watching a movie and I was supposed to be in my room studying. Yeah, it all went through my head as I hung there waiting to die."

Cass shared how the first few seconds after hitting rocks from falling off the cliff were excruciating from the skull fracture, but then the pain dissipated to nothing. “That’s when I arrived here. Like a flash. Wearing this hideous white polo.”

I can relate to that girl. I don't remember feeling pain so I can rule out a cliff fall as the cause of my death. I’m not into hiking in the first place.

Allister shared his death as a feeling of, “small pieces of you painstakingly being chipped away until there is nothing left. Cancer sucks.”

None of this is connecting with me. Why can't I remember? Is this some kind of joke being played on me? Where is the hidden camera? Why can they all remember, but I can't?

Tracy had graduated from Group.

I envy Tracy right now.

The only memory Jade had about her death was the nothingness. Nothing hurt, nothing showed up to tell her where to go, nothing flashed before her eyes. She remembered Adelaide explaining to her that once an individual comes to terms with their death, they are able to progress and move on.

I wish I could see my family right now. It would make this whole experience less atrocious.

Ezekiel fidgeted in his seat. “Pressure. I remember a lot of pressure. I didn’t die right away. One second, I was completely healthy, and the next I was lying in a pool of my own blood, bleeding out, telling myself it would all be over soon. It didn't feel as long as your experience, Jerome, but it didn't happen quickly."

Bled out? From what? A gunshot? A knife attack? A fall off a bridge? Maybe he was heading to a family party or home from school. Maybe he…

Jade listened in more, waiting to hear if he gave specifics of his death. Ezekiel did not share details beyond that he and his friend were riding in a car at night.

Damn it.

……

Jade spent a lot of time with Ezekiel outside of Group. They frequently walked the rose gardens, discussed college baseball, and which celebrity would play them in a movie about their lives. Ezekiel told dad jokes, and Jade impressed with goofy dance skills. He enjoyed banana pancakes from the cafeteria commons, and she enjoyed the hotdogs from the cart in Center Square. Ezekiel shared that he was the middle child of seven kids growing up in Southern California. Around Jade's age as well, Ezekiel planned on attending college in the coming year. "Go Bruins." He frequently chimed in.

"My parents wanted me to go to Berkeley as my mother did, but Boston had a better lacrosse team. Plus, I've always wanted to live on the East Coast, and the opportunity presented itself, so I took it."

"How did your parents take the news?"

Horribly.

"Fine, I guess. They were happy that I planned to attend college. My brother played football for the University of Oregon and Pearl was heading to Cambridge. Smarty-pants McGee."

"Wow, sounds like your family is college-smarts heavy."

"Nah, more like super focused."

"Two of my older brothers were attending college in Utah. No athletes, but one was studying acting and the other nuclear biology."

"That's pretty legit."

"You want to know something completely inappropriate?"

"Let's hear it, Zeek."

"If our situations hadn't happened to us, then we would have never met. Right?"

As bad as it sounds, he's got a point.

"I would have been in Los Angeles, and you would have been in Boston. The likelihood of our paths crossing would have been slim to none," Ezekiel said. "I find you very interesting, Jade."

"Math is my worst subject, Zeek. Configuring probability makes my head hurt."

“Of all the bad mistakes I’ve made, the one mistake that brought me to you might have been the only one worth it.”

“Mistake?”

What mistake could he have possibly made?

His cobalt blue eyes retracted to the ground, and he became mute.

“What do you mean by mistake, Zeek?” Jade continued.

“I… I… I don’t want to talk about it right now, Jade,” Ezekiel said. “Someday, though. Okay?”

Okay, now I really want to know.

“Okay.”

“Let’s walk, what do you say?”

“Sure. I have to meet Adelaide this afternoon, though.”

“Progress checkup?”

“Yep. I’ve got a spirit mom. Who would have known?” Jade said.

“She’s trying to help,” Ezekiel said.

“Yeah, yeah, I know. Put in the time, and work and I’ll get where I need to go, eh.”

“Do you think we will see each other when we move on?” Ezekiel asked.

I sure hope so.

“Good question. If we find each other, I think we will be fine. I mean how big can it be?”

"My guess is pretty big. Probably bigger than this." Ezekiel stretched his arms out.

"Stop. I know it's big. But you know, 'It's a small world' type deal."

"Ha. Yes, I do."

"You make me smile and laugh, Zeek."

……

"Good afternoon, Jade," Adelaide greeted as she rose from her desk upon Jade's arrival. "How are things going?"

"Oh, you know, dead at times," Jade said.

Adelaide's flat expression relayed her unimpressed reaction. "Do you feel as though you have made progress in Group? You've attended a handful of sessions now. Any headway to share?"

"There is this boy. And we are getting along great."

"Honey, it's nice you are making friends, but I would like to focus on your *personal progress* through the program."

"This is progress for me."

"Your focus right now should be on *you*."

Adelaide stood there with her hands on her hips, tapping her right index finger. "Wait outside for a minute. I need to make a quick call."

Confused by the sudden dismissal, Jade abided by Adelaide's wishes, did an about-face, and exited the door she had entered into a few minutes prior. She waited outside for what seemed like forever, which turned out to be just forty-five seconds when Adelaide opened the door and invited her back inside.

"Okay," Adelaide started. "I don't usually do this until better progress has been made, but I'm sticking my neck out here to help get you back on track. You only get three chances, so it's up to you if you want to use one or not."

"Depends what you mean by 'chance.'"

"You will be able to visit your family, under my supervision, of course, so nothing goes astray. The point of this is to help you see why you are working to move on. Why you don't want to remain here," Adelaide said.

"What's wrong with wanting to stay here?" "We've had this conversation before. Complete your work so you can move on. Is seeing your family something you want to do?"

"Yes! Oh yes. I would love to see my family. When can we do this? Can we go now? How long can I stay?"

"Whoa, okay, okay," Adelaide said. "There are a few things you will need to know. One, we do have a time limit. We can only stay for ten minutes for the first visit. Two, they will not be able to see or hear you, so attempting to communicate will not be beneficial. Three, stay with me. This is new for you, and any disturbance you try to make will result in immediate departure. Clear?"

"You got it."

"One last warning that you must abide by. If you fail to follow protocol or do not stay the entire visit for any reason, you will lose your next visit. No exceptions."

"Roger."

"Good. We will leave in the morning. Go get some sleep."

Jade's heart beat at a tremendous rate as she ran down the hall to her room. She grew more excited by the second, knowing she would soon see her family.

I'm so excited to see Mom, Dad, Jamie, Andrew, and, most of all, Pearl.

As Jade calmed, she slipped into a heavy slumber.

I can't wait to see Pearl. Tomorrow is going to be a great day.

She glanced over and caught her clock at 11:11, then closed her eyes.

"Yes, it will be."

FOUR

Pearl hunched over gasping for air as "American Idiot" blasted in her earbuds. "A melody to my death as my body gives out right now," Pearl shared with Jamie, who jogged in place while she caught her breath.

"Come on, sis, Dr. Lenowitz recommended exercise to get those endorphins going. You're doing great, a little bit left."

"Dude, we've run two miles already. You're killing me here."

"You can stop if you want. Giving up is easier than pushing through, but it's up to you."

"Dang it!" Pearl straightened her posture upright and began running in place, then sprinted out in front of Jamie like a wind-up doll cranked up and let go.

"Wait up!" Jamie shouted. But Pearl kept running faster

and harder than she had ever run in her life. Jamie caught a glimpse of a smile from Pearl when she looked back at him as if to say, "ha ha, I'm beating you." He'd take the defeat if it made Pearl smile.

Pearl stopped at the corner and waited for the walk signal.

Skateboard wheels screeched against the asphalt and then came to an abrupt stop. Pearl paid no attention to the sound, staring forward with a flat expression.

"I need to talk to you," Henry said.

Silence.

"Pearl, can you hear me? I need to talk to you."

Silence.

"Pearl."

Silence.

"Please forgive me, Pearl. I didn't know what I gave her. Someone must have switched it on me."

Pearl slowly pivoted her head in Henry's direction, her eyes piercing through him, but said nothing.

"What the hell are you doing talking to her? Get away from her!" Jamie shouted as he pushed Henry out of the way.

"Pearl, you have to believe me!" Henry pleaded. "I didn't know. Please, forgive me."

Jamie grabbed Pearl by her shoulders and leaned forward. "You okay?" he whispered.

Pearl nodded. The two then ran across the intersection in a sprint.

Pearl could hear the echoing sound of Henry's plea, "Forgive me, Pearl! Please, forgive me!" as distance made his pleas softer and softer.

His voice is like glass on my temple. I can't hear this anymore.

Pearl shook her head to dislodge the sound from her brain, but to no avail.

"Can you believe the nerve of that asshole?" Jamie said. "He contributed to our sister's death and has the nerve to say he's sorry? That son of a bitch. That son of a bitch. Son of a bitch."

Pearl placed her hand on Jamie's forearm. "Jamie… it's okay,"

"I'm fine," he said as he pulled his arm from Pearl's grasp.

Silence accompanied them on the remainder of their jog.

……

Pearl went straight to her room when she got home and retrieved a piece of stationary, pulled her red pen from the case, and wrote, "I don't blame you, Henry" in the middle of the page. Pearl then folded the paper in half, eight times, placed it back in her desk drawer, and headed to the bathroom to shower off the sweaty stench she had accumulated on her jog.

"How was your jog, darling?" Marlene asked as she intercepted Pearl in the hallway.

Oh god. Not now.

"Fine, Mom. I survived."

"Okay," Marlene murmured, stepping aside to allow Pearl passage to the bathroom. "I'm here if you need anything," she said as Pearl shut the door to the bathroom, terminating their interaction.

Pearl stepped into the chilly shower. Initially, she flinched as the cold temperature shot from the shower head. She reached for the hot water handle then stopped herself.

If I stay in the cold water long enough, maybe I will get pneumonia.

She proceeded to slide the glass door shut, shivering. For fifteen minutes, Pearl stood in the shower, not washing her hair or body. just standing, engulfed by the cold water that the shower head produced.

FIVE

Jade and Ezekiel sat on the wood bench, placed in the center of the rose garden, enjoying the evening before Jade's first visit to see her family.

"I'm nervous."

"About what?"

"I don't know. But I feel nervous."

"Hmmmm, let's see what the cause could be. You haven't seen your family in a while, right?"

Obvious.

Jade nodded

"Are you nervous about any change?"

"Change?"

"Yes, change as in a family-dynamic change. Whether they will seem happy or whether they will all seem sad that you are gone."

"Happy that I'm gone? Wow."

"Wait, no. That's not what I meant. I meant they wouldn't be sad that you are gone. No. I mean…ugh, it's not coming out how I am thinking it should."

Does that foot taste good in your mouth Zeek?

"Relax, Zeek, I know what you meant."

Ezekiel's right. If they did seem happy without me, as if I never existed, I'm not sure I could handle it. Would it affect my progress if they are like this when I see them?

"Maybe I shouldn't go."

"Oh, heck no. You should *definitely* go. I know it helped my progress to see my family."

"How did your first visit go?"

He made no eye contact with Jade as he spoke about his experience. "Mom was sad, so were my siblings. People were asking, "Why… why… why..." I visited during their support group, which helped me because I was able to hear my parents' thoughts and feelings about my death."

This, I must hear.

"And… how did they feel?"

Ezekiel paused for a few seconds, then glanced at Jade, sorrow filling his eyes. "Guilty, and like failures over what I had done."

How awful.

"At first, it was bad seeing them like that, but as the session went along, I witnessed guilt fading from them, and I think that's what helped me." His expression transformed from sorrow to elated.

"How did it help?"

"It gave me warmth. It's hard seeing family members suffer because of choices you made."

I hope this isn't what my family is going through right now. "I feel you on that. But wait, 'as the session went along?' You mean, you were there for more than ten minutes?"

"Yes. That was my second visit. If your first visit goes well, then your second one is much longer. Make tomorrow count, okay?"

Jade blinked her eyes rapidly. "Yep. Will do. What did happen to you? You never shared it in Group."

"Soon. So, your family. Two siblings, right?"

Jade narrowed her eyes and pursed her lips.

Avoiding the subject. Clever.

After a few seconds, she surrendered to Ezekiel's request. "Three."

"Three. Where do you sit in line?"

"Tied for second."

"Tied for second? I'm not following."

"I have a twin, Pearl. We are second in line behind our brother Jamie. We also have a younger brother, Andrew. I didn't tell you that Pearl and I were twins?"

"Nope."

Way to go, Jade.

"We were. Thick as thieves. Always had each other's back."

"Sounds awesome. So, is she as beautiful as you?"

Jade's cheeks blushed. "Zeek, stop. Yes, she is. In my opinion, she's more. She has the prettiest black hair."

"Black hair? It's not red like yours? How is that possible?"

Jade laughed, "Mom is Irish, and Dad is Mexican. Let's say in vitro fertilization went better than planned —one olive-skinned redhead, one ivory-skinned raven-head. We spent our whole lives explaining to people that we were twins, but most of the time, they didn't believe us. 'The Juarez un-twins' became our unofficial title. Not clever in the slightest, if you ask me."

……

Her tight grip turned her knuckles white as nervousness kicked in. Jade glanced down at her baby blue Chucks, the sparkly silver in her laces dancing in the sunlight. Pearl hinged her wrist with Jade's grip and smiled, reciprocating a smirk. Fourth grade at a new school seemed scary. Jade pulled the collar of her canary yellow polo, loosening the constriction from the school uniform she now had to wear.

"You two are going to do great. This is one of the best schools around, and everyone is going to love you," Jeff said.

"I don't know anybody, Daddy."

"You know *me*. That's a start," Pearl said.

"Ugh. Why do we have to go here again? What was wrong with our last school?"

"Well, Mija, it's further away from Mommy's new job, and my coworker recommended this school."

"Just give it a try. Private school may be a little different, but the teachers are nice, and you are going to learn so much," Marlene said.

"What does private even mean?" Jade asked. "School is school."

"How bad can it be? Let's go, sis," Pearl said.

Jade reluctantly followed Pearl's lead and proceeded through the tall metal gate labeled, "ALBATROSS ACADEMY. WHERE STUDENTS SOAR."

Mrs. Baxter greeted the girls at room fifteen. Her inviting smile gestured them in as she announced, "Attention class. I would like to introduce our new classmates, the Juarez sisters, Jade and Pearl. Let's show them our Albatross best and help make them feel welcome."

"Sisters?" a voice in the back said.

Jade fidgeted her collar.

"I don't get it. You look nothing alike. Is one of you adopted?"

Pearl laughed, "That's funny. No, we are twins. "Fraternal" is what we are called. I can do a presentation one day to explain it. Can I, Mrs. Baxter?"

"Sure, Pearl, that would be lovely and educational," Mrs. Baxter said.

"Nerd," Jade whispered to Pearl. The sisters exchanged a smile.

Classmates smiled, some giggled, others raised eyebrows, curious about what the word "fraternal" meant.

……

"She had always been a bookworm," Jade said.

"And you?" Ezekiel asked.

"I got the grades, but sports were more my gig."

"Anything is possible."

"Hey, I got into Boston U, so I didn't do too bad."

"Ha. Valid point. Definitely a bucket list item I will sorely miss not experiencing."

"Maybe in the next life."

"If you believe that. Full disclosure. I feel I need to express something to you. You have made me realize that I can recover."

"How so?"

"There's a light in you. You want to heal; I can see that. But you are stuck. I was stuck, like you. Not sure how to feel, or act, or what to even do next. I arrived shortly before you did. Looking at you now, I realize I have come farther than I thought I did. Thank you."

Not sure why I need to be thanked. "You're welcome?"

"Honey, look… you've shown me that I have progressed, and I like that. I want the same for you. Progress, please, for you."

Honey?

"Please, Jade?"

"I'm working on it. I just need to get some facts squared away before I can get to that point, okay?"

"Fine. I'll be watching you."

Well, that would be lovely. "Awesome."

……

Jade rose from her bed and examined herself in the mirror.

Lucky for me, there are no bad hair days here.

She tousled her fingers through her curly mane and set out the door to meet up with Adelaide.

Adelaide was sitting in her office, writing notes when Jade arrived. "Are we ready to go?" Jade asked. Her eyes were bright with a smile to match.

"Wrapping up a few things here, then we will be all set."

Jade waited in the hall while Adelaide completed her work. She jumped from her seat when the office door opened, and Adelaide's head poked out in peekaboo-like fashion. "Ready to go, Jade?"

"Oh, hell yeah," Jade said, her comment met with a flat and stern glance from Adelaide. "Oh sorry. I meant—oh, heck yeah." Adelaide's face fixed to a smile.

Adelaide reached into the rustic brown leather satchel draped over her shoulder and pulled out a large heart-shaped amulet whose delicate silver necklace chain tumbled out behind it. Blush pink, as the roses from the garden, and hugged by a layer of red stone, it's beauty mesmerized Jade as she reached out to touch it. She paused only to absorb the fortress of metal thorns encasing its shape as though they were created solely to protect the heirloom from harm.

"This will help us complete our visit today. This stone is special and needs to be handled in the most delicate of ways. It is the only one you will have, Jade, so please be careful with it. It can be used for visitation purposes, but can also be used to see visions of those close to you when you're not on a visit. Does this make sense?"

"You mean, like a crystal ball or something?" Jade

questioned.

I could check on anyone at any time. This is great.

"Yes, something like that. But if it gets cracked or breaks, it becomes completely useless and will not work. There is no way to replace it. So, if this happens, all contact will be lost with your family for good."

"Gotcha. Be careful with it. Can we go now?"

"Easy, Jade," Adelaide said. "Remember, you only have ten minutes for this visit. Also, wherever you decide to go, you must stay there for the full ten minutes. You cannot change and go to another location. It's kind of a one-stop deal, okay?"

Jade nodded.

"Okay. Where would you like to go?"

"Home. Everyone should be there having morning breakfast."

"Okay, home it is then. Now, hold this in your hand and think about home. Don't think about the people, think about the place."

Jade closed her eyes and stated her address, "579 Daisy Lane."

She opened her eyes and stood in the center of the kitchen. A brisk thrust of air penetrated her chest as Marlene walked through her on the way to the dining room table.

Wow, it worked.

Adelaide giggled and rolled her eyes. "Of course, it did."

Familiar scents hit Jade's nose. The smell of eggs and chorizo mixed with vanilla sugar-scented candles choked her up as she smiled. She was back home.

I'm invisible, but I'm back.

Marlene chatted with Andrew while he ate before heading to the skate park for his regular hangout session with friends. Jamie sat on the couch, reading the professional football scouting report. Jeff sat at the island in the kitchen, complimenting Marlene on how great the eggs tasted. Jade quickly scanned the room and didn't notice Pearl sitting anywhere.

"Where's Pearl?" Jade asked.

Adelaide shrugged her shoulders.

"Do you think she'll come out today, Mom?" Andrew asked.

Jade's head swiveled to her brother.

Come out today?

Jade glanced back to Adelaide, who raised her eyebrows and shrugged her shoulders a second time.

"I'm not sure, Andrew. Maybe we will be lucky."

"After the Henry incident, I wouldn't be surprised if she never comes out."

"Andrew."

Henry incident? "What are they talking about?"

Adelaide sighed, "I am not informed of what happens in the living unless it will directly impact your progress."

"This sucks. I can't talk to them? I need to know what they are talking about."

"I know it's frustrating, dear, but try your best to stay focused."

How can I focus when I don't know what they are talking about?

Jade didn't listen to Adelaide. She ran to the stairs and proceeded up to Pearl's room.

I only have a few more minutes.

"Jade," Adelaide cautioned. "Wait." But Jade didn't hear. Or didn't want to hear. She ran as fast as she could up the first seven steps followed by a quick left turn and seven more steps until she found herself on the second floor, holding onto the bannister, catching her breath. Jade stood, staring at Pearl's bedroom door. She could feel her heart beating in her ears. Adelaide watched as Jade attempted to open the door, but to no avail.

"You can't open the door, sweetie. But you can go through it," she said, hoping Jade's ears caught the message.

Jade paused.

What am I going to find on the other side of this door? What will Pearl look like? Will she be reading, or writing, or texting her crush? Maybe, doing some drawing?

Jade was ready to find out. She took a step forward, then another, and then reached for the doorknob. Her hand unsuccessfully gripped the knob as it swept through it. "Crap," Jade blurted out. "I forgot; I can't move objects."

"THROUGH the door, Jade," Adelaide said as she finally made it to the top of the stairs. "Haven't you seen any ghost movies?"

Jade glanced over at Adelaide with a devilish smirk. "Duh."

Jade took three steps into complete darkness. Not knowing whether to move or not, her vision escaped her for a few seconds until a sound emerged. She glanced towards her two o'clock and heard the sound again. A low, quiet, and soft breath could be heard. Pearl was in her room. Sleeping.

Why is she sleeping this late? "I can't see anything."

"You're stuck, darling, you can't turn on the lights. You are just going to have to listen. You only have about a minute left," Adelaide said.

"Ugh, this is annoy–"

"It's not your fault," Pearl whispered.

Jade stopped in her tracks. "What was that, Pearl?"

"It's not your fault," Pearl said again.

"What's not your fault?" Jade questioned.

"It's not your fault."

"What does she mean?"

"I don't know," Adelaide whispered into the darkness.

"It's not your fault."

What is she talking about?

"I don't understand. What does she mean, Adelaide?"

"It's not your fault, Pearl."

"'Not your fault, Pearl?' What is she talking about, Adelaide?"

Wide-eyed, Adelaide had no response.

"It's okay, Pearl, I'm here," Jade said.

Pearl began sobbing.

"It's okay." Jade reached out over the bed and knelt to her knees to embrace Pearl's shoulders. Her arms went through Pearl's body. Jade's hands clenched.

"What kind of crap is this, Adelaide? I only get ten minutes, and I don't even get to see her? What a waste of time."

"I'm sorry, sweetie. I know it's hard, but time has expired, and we need to go."

No. Not now.

Jade remained at Pearl's bedside, gripping the amulet around her neck as she comforted her sister with a free hand. Adelaide approached Jade and wrapped her arms around her, "It's going to be okay. I know it's frustrating right now. The first time usually is. You want more time, which is normal. We all do. But, for now, we must go. You will see her again soon. Come on, Jade, give me the amulet."

"No. I need to know what she means."

"You won't find out today. And you won't find out next time if you choose not to follow the rules and give me the amulet right now. I'm sorry about this."

"But…"

"The amulet, please."

Jade surrendered her grip on the amulet, and in one slow swoop, laced the chain between her fingers and guided it off from around her neck. Jade handed the amulet to Adelaide, who then held Jade close and closed her eyes.

They were back at welcoming quarters.

Jade left Adelaide's embrace and continued down the hall to her room. Jade said nothing to Adelaide as the distance between them grew greater and greater. Jade opened the door and turned on the light switch. "Figures, I can turn on the light when it doesn't matter." She threw herself on the bed. Her eyelids became heavier and heavier by the second. Jade didn't bother to turn the lights off before she went to sleep. She found herself repeatedly whispering, "It's not your fault, Pearl," until the stillness of night took over the sound of her whispers.

SIX

"I'm trying to be here. Doesn't that mean anything?" Pearl said as the rest of the group studied her emotions.

Always judging me.

She sat there expressionless as Albert asked her the mind-cringing weekly check-in questions.

"Yes, I'm still sad."

"No, I haven't dealt with her death."

"No, I'm not ready to talk about it."

I hate this group.

Pearl became auto-tuned to screen out stories by other members every session. Each week presented a tale emotionally heavier than its predecessor, which didn't help Pearl with her recovery. The only other teen in the group was a boy named Sander. They made eye contact a few times prior. Sander shared his struggle working through the death of his only sibling. His brother had died while the two of them were out with friends one night. Pearl understood the story—the brother played chicken on the highway after Sander pleaded with him to stop. Sander did not finish his story, but Pearl knew exactly how it ended. For the first time in weeks, she found somebody she could relate to—someone who would understand her predicament, who could be the key to her healing.

"You look like you could use a friend," Sander said, following Group.

Captain obvious here.

"Is it obvious?"

"Come with me. I know a great place that makes the best coffee that'll make your taste buds sing."

"What place?"

"It's called 'Cup O' Joes.' My friend's parents own the place."

What does that have to do with anything?

"You interested? You seem hesitant. I promise you'll like it. It's got a great ambiance."

What could it hurt?

She gave a quick nod, and the two began the five-block journey. Pearl sent her mother a text during the venture:

PEARL: BE HOME LATER. GOING FOR COFFEE WITH

SANDER.

MOM: SANDER?

PEARL: YES, FROM GROUP.

MOM: OK. LOVE YOU BUNCHES.

PEARL: BUNCHES BACK.

Cup O Joe's café sat on the corner of Fifth and Market. The aroma sent Pearl's senses into overdrive as she took in the scent of freshly brewed coffee beans, exotic tea blends, and fresh cinnamon. Eight small tables decorated the café—half round, half square. Each only large enough to hold two people. Jazz music played faintly in the background, strengthening the calming ambiance. The walls were splattered with vintage photographs of glamorous legends of the silver screen dating back to the early 1930s.

How adorable.

Pearl felt transported to a time of simplicity. She studied the menu before approaching the gentleman in the bow tie and suspenders who greeted them when they arrived.

"What'll you order there?" He asked.

"Coffee, please. Black. No sugar, no cream."

"Ladies and gents, we've got a rebel in the house. Going hardcore with your coffee, girl. I like your style."

If he only knew.

Pearl cracked a side smile as Sander bumped her shoulder

with his and giggled at the notion.

"Whoa, hold on a second. Is that a smile I see poking out from those beautiful lips of yours?" Sander said, half shocked.

"Maybe."

"Yesssss. Sander has done it. My life is complete. I shall need no more from this day forward to make me happy, as I have accomplished the Mount Everest of all tasks in life. I have made Pearl smile."

She backhanded his outer thigh. Her face straightened as she narrowed her eyebrows. "Stop. You joke as if I never smile."

"You don't, my dear," he said as he rubbed his leg to relieve the sting from Pearl's whack.

Pearl didn't respond. Her coffee was ready, and she darted over to the counter to pick up her order.

I hope he doesn't plan to continue poking fun at my happiness level—Total buzzkill.

"Shall we?" Sander announced as he motioned for Pearl to sit at the small round table near the front window.

Pearl led the way to the table, sitting down with her back facing the window. Sander shrugged as he sat next to her and placed his white teacup with a blue dancing bear pattern on the designated coaster.

What's with the shrug?

"Not interested in facing the world outside?" Sander

asked.

"Me? No. I just don't want people watching me while I drink my coffee."

"Unlike you, sweetie, I prefer to sit at an angle where I can see what is happening outside."

Pearl paid no attention to Sander's comment. She found herself staring at a dancing bear on his teacup, imagining that her glance would cause it to dance right off the cup. Still staring at the bear, she brought her mug to her chin and inhaled the fresh aroma as it tickled her senses with the smell, awakening her mood on the warm Portland afternoon.

"How long ago did your sister move on?"

Too soon guy. "Move on?"

"Yes, move on. I prefer that term instead of 'die.' To me, it seems less permanent. Like, when something dies, that's it, there's nothing left of it but rot and emptiness. Some say that when a person dies, their body is a vessel that is left behind, and their spirit moves on. That's why I prefer say 'move on' instead of 'die.'"

"Does it help you cope?"

"We create what helps us cope. So, yes, it helps me."

Sander blinked his eyes slowly as he fixed his vision on a dancing bear on his teacup, tracing his fingers along the side of the cup. Pearl watched as if he drew an invisible path for the bear to follow. But it didn't follow. He took a slow, deep breath out, and with a smile on his face, looked up at Pearl.

"What were you involved in at school?" He asked.

"What?"

"School. You know, the place you attend that has people and teachers and clubs. Were you involved in anything?"

"Student government."

"And Jade?"

How did he know her name?

Sander stumbled his speech. "That is your sister, right?"

"I don't remember saying her name when you were in Group."

"You… didn't. Jamie did. I asked around too."

"You were asking about me?"

"Gosh, when you say it that way, I sound like a creeper."

"I'm not implying anything…."

"I was curious, Pearl. Everyone else shares their story except you, so I asked around. Finally, someone gave me some intel. There, satisfied?"

No. "Sure."

Pearl receded to her mug and took a sip of the happiness that had been brewed inside just for her.

Maybe this will absorb into me and pep me up.

She jumped as Sander reached his hand out to her and

touched the top of her wrist. An alien sensation came over her as she loosened her grip on the mug. Her neck and chest flushed. Her eyes locked with Sander's, and his smile comforted her. She smiled back. Another feeling came over her. Humor. Pearl giggled.

"Something got your funny bone?"

"Sort of. Just a random thought popped into my head."

"Care to share?"

"It's silly, really. Just something that happened between Jade and me."

"Oh, this I've got to hear," Sander said, continuing to sip his beverage.

"Oh, alright. Lost Lake, a few summers back...."

……

Pearl always avoided jumping into the water. Fear gripped her every summer her family visited Lost Lake Campground. She knew how to swim, but her inability to see the bottom of the lake always made her uneasy. She enjoyed lounging on the boat and sunbathing on the shore, but never swam in the water. Jade pleaded every summer for her to jump off the boat into the lake, but to no avail. This summer, they agreed to jump in on the count of three.

"You ready for this? Don't get scared again."

"I promise you. Count of three, right?"

"Right."

They began counting. "One, two…" before Pearl got to three, Jade wrapped her arms around Pearl's waist, lifted her feet off the ground, and plunged into the lake with Pearl in tow.

"Oh my god!" Pearl scolded, bobbing in the water as she gasped for air.

"What? Now you've jumped in the lake. My job here is finished."

Pearl splashed Jade in the face, then swam back to the boat. "We were supposed to go on three, Jade. You totally threw me off. I wasn't expecting that!"

"Literally and figuratively," Jade said, winking at her sister.

Pearl rolled her eyes. She scolded Jade for the stunt and didn't talk to her for half of the day.

……

"That's a funny story. Your sister sounds like she was quite the character."

Pearl quickly pulled her hand from Sander's touch. "How could I have hated her for trying to help?"

"Help with what?"

Pearl quickly became aware that her inner monologue had failed her. "Nothing," she replied as she returned her attention to her coffee. "Where are you from? This area? Somewhere magical?"

Sander smiled. "Quite the sense of humor you have. Yes, in my life, I have lived in a series of magical places, so it's difficult to pinpoint where I am from."

"Wow. Where have you lived? Unfortunately, I have lived in places no further than the county lines. Maybe someday I'll go somewhere else."

"Oh, you know, a little in Europe, a little in Asia, around the states…"

"Gotcha."

"You wanna go for a stroll?"

"Sure. I could use some sun."

"Yes, you can."

"Sander," Pearl hackled as she smacked on his left arm.

Rubbing his arm as if Pearl inflicted some amount of pain, Sander rose from his seat, reaching for the coffee mug and bear teacup, "I'll take these." Pearl examined the teacup as the bears danced out of her sight.

If I could dance away like those bears, nobody will even notice. I can disappear, and nobody will realize I was gone. Right, easier said than done."

"Ready?"

No. "Yes."

……

Dinner began with a quiet tone. Pearl engaged in her usual somber banter with her food. She kept scooting and sliding it in infinite motion. Her food was barely eaten.

"Maybe a few bites tonight?"

"Mom."

"Sorry. Continue."

"Continue?"

"Never mind."

"No, Mom, you obviously have something on your mind. Get to it."

Marlene studied the slice of pork roast on her fork, then focused her attention on Pearl. She lowered her fork to her plate, her breath matching her motion, deep and labored.

"Look, Pearl. We miss you. We miss how you were. How you were before Jade… how you were. You hardly ever come out of your room anymore, and when you do, you don't talk to any of us. You go to Group and then spend hours out doing who knows what. I'm worried about you, sweetie. We all are."

Jeff sat silently, but Pearl knew he agreed with Marlene.

Andrew rose from the table and threw his napkin down. "You're selfish, Pearl! This isn't about you. We all miss Jade. It didn't just happen to you; it happened to all of us. So stop being self-centered and move on already."

"Andrew." Marlene interrupted, but he was already

rushing upstairs to his bedroom.

"I'm sorry to be such a downer to you all. I will show myself to the cave. Good evening."

"You don't have to leave, honey. Please stay and finish dinner."

"I'm not hungry."

"Pearl. We love you," Marlene said, hoping the words landed with her intended sincerity.

Pearl stopped for a moment but failed to turn around and acknowledge her mother's endearment. She proceeded up the stairs, down the hall, and into her bedroom. The door slammed with an echo that shook the house. Marlene glanced over to Jeff, who remained silent at the table.

"I don't know what to do anymore, Jeff. I can't seem to get through to her, and Group isn't helping. Whenever I see her, she's either angry at me or she's ignoring me. To remember her smile, I have to look at old photographs, and it's upsetting to know she isn't that girl anymore."

"She lost her twin, Marlene," Jeff said in a whisper. "Do you remember how I was when I lost Samuel? I was forty-five. I couldn't imagine going through that when I was seventeen. I think, in time, she will figure out how to cope. It will take time. It has only been a few months. We can't expect a miracle overnight."

Marlene collapsed her head into her palms and began sobbing. "I miss our daughters."

Jeff embraced Marlene. "She'll come back. You'll see."

……

Pearl threw herself onto the bed and cried.

Nobody understands what I'm going through here. Except Sander.

Pearl retrieved her phone and opened the text bubble.

PEARL: Hey. What are you doing?

SANDER: Hanging here. What's up?

PEARL: Nothing. Got into it with my mom.

SANDER: Parents. What a drag sometimes. You

OK?

PEARL: Whatever, I'm over it.

SANDER: What did you fight about?

PEARL: Oh, the usual. I'm emo and they don't like

that I am not all chipper since my twin died.

SANDER: I know what you mean.

PEARL: You seem to get me. Thank you.

SANDER: Hey, no problem kid.

PEARL: Kid?

SANDER: LOL sorry, I mean, girl.

PEARL: Sometimes I wish I wasn't here anymore.

SANDER: So, move out.

PEARL: Not here. Here.

SANDER: Explain.

PEARL:

SANDER: Pearl?

PEARL:

SEVEN

Jade sat in Group, twiddling her thumbs and rapidly bouncing the balls of her feet. She no longer had sensation in her bottom lip from her top teeth pinning it down so hard. She couldn't get the visit off her mind—not seeing Pearl, the way her family spoke about Pearl. Frustration was pent up inside her, and she was ready to burst. She needed to say something.

"Jade, I notice you seem to be a little tense today. Everything okay?" Chase asked.

"Dandy."

"Hmmm, I sense some sarcasm in your tone. Anything you want to discuss?"

No.

Ezekiel nudged her foot with his. Jade released the tension inside with a heavy breath.

"I went on my first family visit yesterday."

"Oh?"

"Yes."

"And?"

"I'm sitting here shaking like a weirdo, aren't I?"

"Do you mind me asking what about the visit contributed to how you feel today?" Chase asked.

"Yes, actually, I do."

"Fair enough. Okay, Group, let's start by…"

"Wait," Jade said. "I visited my family during breakfast." Jade proceeded to share details about the visit.

"I would be lying if I said that Pearl wasn't my main reason for the visit. I really wanted to see her, but I couldn't, and that was frustrating."

"Couldn't?"

Here we go. "Yes, couldn't. I went to her room, and the lights were out. Like, pitch-black dark. I couldn't see anything, but I could hear her breathing, and repeating over and over, 'It's not your fault.' I had no idea what she meant. The whole experience frustrated me because I couldn't talk to her or anybody. All I could do was endure the silent torture."

"I'm sorry your first visit did not go according to plan. One thing all the group members here agree on is, sometimes, life doesn't go according to plan, which can be extremely frustrating. Have you been able to think about your second visit yet?"

"No. I freaked out during this one. I think my second one may be canceled."

"Oh. Adelaide will work this out with you."

Jade locked her lips once more as she sat there thinking about when she would want to visit her family next.

There's every Thursday for movie night or Sunday morning after church. Or maybe…

Then it hit her. Jade kicked Ezekiel in his ankle. He winced at the initial sting and exchanged glances with her, confirming her message. Jade leaned her head slightly to the right and whispered, "Group."

"Huh?"

"Group. I'll go when she is in Group."

"Whatever floats your boat."

Jade left the session with a smile on her face.

I'm ready now. Ready to see my family again—ready to see my sister and not be left in the dark.

……

"What would going during Group help you with?" Ezekiel asked.

"Information. It's what I need. Last time, she was alone, which didn't tell me much. Maybe if I visit her in an environment where she is speaking with others, she will say something useful."

"Like how you died?"

"Yes, it could give me some insight."

"Sounds like a good idea. Be sure to stay focused, so you can progress through the program. Not all of us stay here forever."

"What's that supposed to mean?"

"Nothing. Don't take your time."

"I'm not following. What are you getting at?"

Ezekiel exhaled sharply, staring into his lap. "Look, Jade. The purpose of us being here is to work on progressing through the program so we can move on. You don't seem to be doing what you need to do for that to happen. You are too caught up with Pearl and are not focusing on yourself. Do you even want to move on?"

"What are you saying, Zeek?"

"I… I don't know. I don't know."

You better be going somewhere with this.

"Fancy you saying that since you are still here."

"It's different for me."

"How? From what I can tell, if you are here, it's because you haven't progressed. So, what's your deal?"

"I don't have one."

Ezekiel's head redirected to his left and focused on the grass as he fidgeted his hands in his lap.

"If you have something to say to me, just say it."

"It doesn't matter. Just do what you need to do to get things done."

"Why? What will happen if I don't? Do you know what happens if we don't?"

"I've heard things."

"Like what?"

"No one really knows where we go when we progress. Some have said we stay right here. Others have said we go somewhere that isn't pleasant. I don't know what to believe, so I'm just focusing on finishing."

"Oh."

"You okay?"

Jade collected herself. "Am I okay? Besides for being dead, I would say I'm dandy."

"Right," Ezekiel said. "You look like you are going to upchuck."

Upchuck sounds about right.

Her stomach twisted and churned, and her cheeks flushed with warmth. She was uncertain whether the choices she had made in her progress would leave her stuck there forever. She valued everything Ezekiel had told her during her stay, even the harsh truths. She considered him a good friend. Another wave of nausea rushed through her intestines.

What if I don't see him after I pass on? How gut-wrenching would that be?

EIGHT

Pearl became accustomed to hanging out with Sander daily. She found any excuse she could to be with him; to get out of doing chores, hanging with her family, or attending family functions. Initially, Marlene protested Pearl spending so much time away from family. But she could see how happy it made Pearl, and she didn't want to ruin that.

Pearl and Sander people-watched at the park, had ice cream in the middle of the night, made late-night runs to the local twenty-four-hour diner, and attended the annual Jazz Festival that Sander swore Pearl would like. She didn't care too much for jazz, but she cared for him. A lot.

"Where did you come from?" Pearl asked.

"It's a little complicated," Sander responded.

"Oh, let's hear it."

"When a man and a woman love each other very much, they engage in this activity called 'sex.' Sometimes, the activity creates another human called a 'baby.'" Sander glanced over, caught up in his own humor, to see that Pearl's eyebrows were furrowed, and her lips were pursed. Pearl then smirked as she smacked Sander's bicep with the back of her hand.

"Oh geez, Sander, you're such a dork. Seriously, though, where did you come from? One day you popped in Group like you came out of thin air."

"I came from space. And yes, it hurt when I fell."

Cheesy. "Can I be blunt with you?"

"Of course."

"You help me forget. Forget the pain of losing my sister. Forget the pain of the gaping hole left in my heart. Pain that left me so dark, in an abyss of emotion, that some days, making it out felt like escaping quicksand. You have made my days seem better. I shower more. I smile more, and I know you influenced that. The moments of sadness still outweigh the moments of happiness, but there are more happy moments now. Thank you."

"For what?"

"For what?" Pearl said. "Haven't you noticed I seem different since we started hanging out? That I'm smiling? Wanting to get out of my room and be outside doing stuff? Thank you for contributing to that, Sander."

"Only doing my job."

Job? Am I that much of a burden that it's like a job being with me?

"Pearl? You there?" Sander asked, nudging her on the shoulder. She flickered her eyelids and shook her head, refocusing on Sander's eyes, which steadied below his raised eyebrows.

"What are we going to do today?" Pearl asked.

"Maybe we could do some hiking. How does that sound?"

Crap.

"I know—physical activity. But you can do it. I know you can."

Pearl agreed, and they walked to the late model, two-door hatchback Sander drove around town, buckled in, and headed out for their daily adventure.

The trail hugged a canyon as it weaved in and out of overgrown brush that had grown after the rainy season. Pearl stopped on occasion to catch her breath, but reluctantly continued when Sander grabbed her by the bicep and encouraged her to move on while muttering, "Your lungs need it."

They came upon a lookout point halfway through the trail and sat next to a sharp 100-foot drop. The two stood there silently for a moment, absorbing the environment one breeze at a time. Pearl's eyebrows rose and fell as she teetered forward and back, teasing the cliff with her curiosity.

I wonder if this fall would hurt.

"Whatcha thinking about?"

He wouldn't want to know. Don't scare him, Pearl.

"Pearl?"

"If it would hurt." *Damn it.*

"If what would hurt?"

"The fall."

Sander nervously chuckled. "Are you thinking about finding out?"

Pearl was silent.

"Maybe we should continue."

Sander reached out to grab Pearl's arm, but she pulled away from his clutch and took one step closer to the edge.

"Do you think it will hurt?"

"Of course, it will. It's 100 feet down. Let's go."

"But it wouldn't hurt for long, right? I mean, if I fell, I would most likely break my neck, and it would be over in an instant."

"That's a thought I would rather not ponder in my mind."

"Sometimes…" Pearl started as her eyes traveled down the cliff. Her speech was quiet and hoarse, and her shoulders were slumped. "I don't feel like I can do this anymore," she continued. "Like there is this force I can't control, pulling me, making me feel like I don't need to be here anymore."

"What does it tell you?"

"It doesn't say anything. It feels like an energy."

"Energy."

"A pull. Force. Magnet."

"That's crazy."

"Is it? I've had more moments lately where I'm happy, but when those moments are over, I'm right back at square one. It comes to me like a dark mass that won't leave me alone, that will keep chipping away until there isn't anything left. I feel like I'm losing myself."

"It?"

"The darkness." *The darkness. He doesn't understand. Nobody does.*

Sander slowly approached Pearl and wrapped his arms around her, giving her a soft hug.

"The darkness can't hurt you when I'm around. Now, come on back."

"No. You can't tell me what to do. I will leave when I am ready, okay?"

"Whatever you wish. I'm just trying to…"

"Help? Is that what you are *just* trying to do? Join the club. I'm so over hearing from everyone about how they are trying to help me. All everyone wants to do is help me. I can be helped by being left alone when I want to be left alone. It's suffocating how much you all want to help."

"I was going to say wrap up our walk and head back to your place."

Pearl froze. Embarrassment filled her cheeks with warmth. "If Jade were here, she would crack a joke at me for thinking this way."

"Really? She'd crack a joke about this?"

"Yes. She knew how to lighten the mood with her humor." Pearl thought back to the time Jade attended her debate competition against Willard High.

That crack about child brides. Only Jade could think up something like that.

Pearl smiled. "What time is it?" She asked. Her eyes glazed over as the breeze dried her dewy cheeks.

Sander glanced at his watch but said nothing.

"Time?" Pearl repeated.

"11:15."

Pearl's eyebrows narrowed, and she exhaled, focusing on the empty space three feet in front of her. Her eyes moistened. *So close.*

Sander gave her another gentle squeeze. "Come on, Pearl, we can turn back and go home."

Pearl wiped her eyes. "No. I want to finish," she said,

releasing herself from Sander's embrace. She took a step back from the edge and continued walking along the trail. Sander let out a sharp sigh of relief and followed ten paces behind. As they continued their journey, only the sound of sniffles escaped from Pearl.

……

Silence consumed the car as a thick layer of awkwardness built up between them.

"Have you thought about getting help?" Sander asked.

Nosey. "I have. That's what Group is for."

Sander slowed the vehicle and came to a stop at a red light. He glanced over to Pearl and placed his hand over hers. "I don't like seeing you like this. It makes me sad to see you sad."

"You think I like being this way? What do you take me for?"

"Nothing. I don't mean it that way."

You're not saying anything I don't know. I know something is wrong with me. I know I need help. "I just want to be okay."

"You will be."

"Stop."

"I'm sure Dr. Lenowitz misses you, Pearl. It could help you to talk to…"

"How did you… never mind."

……

Dr. Lenowitz's office felt cold and somber. A collection of vintage child statues were scattered around the office.

So creepy.

Dr. Lenowitz sat behind a large, dark oak desk, which created a lumber moat between Pearl and her, clearly indicating where "doctor" and "patient" sat.

"It's nice to see you again. It feels like it's been a while since we last met. Would you care to update me on what has been happening with you?"

Yes, I do care. Why did I come today?

Pearl fidgeted in her seat and bit her lip. Her skin moistened, and her heart rate accelerated at the thought of discussing her sister.

"I can't sleep."

"How many hours do you sleep a night?" Dr. Lenowitz asked.

Knowing her next statement would be false, Pearl focused her gaze on Dr. Lenowitz's eyes and fixated her stare intently as the lie blurted out, "About two to three hours." Her glance transferred to her shoes as she waited to hear what Dr. Lenowitz would offer as a resolution.

Tools? Medication? Exercise? Answer already.

"What is keeping you up at night?'

"Family, my sister. Stress in general."

"Tell me about that."

"What do you want to know?"

"Define stress. Can you tell me what it physically feels like?"

Focus, girl. "Closing my eyes brings her to life. Knowing she won't come back makes me miserable and anxious. I fear falling asleep because I fear seeing her—knowing she can't be here. So, I don't sleep." Pearl rubbed her forehead. "Does that make sense?"

"Complete sense. So, what I am hearing is that most of your stress comes from your sister's death."

And the fact that I'm responsible for it. "Yes."

"And how does that make you feel?"

"I just said. Tired and stressed."

"I see."

"Sorry."

"It's okay. Do you need something to help you sleep?" Dr. Lenowitz opened the upper right drawer of her desk and pulled out a small pad of paper.

Why isn't she asking more questions?

Pearl studied the paper for a second. A four-by-six-inch pad labeled, "Emma Lenowitz, MD" with an Rx label below.

If I say yes, I will walk out of here with medication. If I say no, I'm left alone to deal with my recovery.

"Yes."

Dr. Lenowitz began writing on the small pad. Her handwriting created artistic grace as the pen danced in circles, barely coming off the paper. Pearl stared, mesmerized at the motions, and smiled at the dance of ink. Dr. Lenowitz noticed the smile on Pearl's face. She placed the pen on her desk and studied intently.

"Tell me how things have been going," Dr. Lenowitz asked.

"You already asked."

Dr. Lenowitz adjusted her red-rimmed glasses as she cleared her throat. "Pearl?"

"Meh."

"Meh?"

"What is it you would like to know? If I'm eating? Going to Group? Whether I cut myself? Or if I miss…" Pearl stopped her monologue and retreated her gaze to her fingers, wrestling with each other in her lap.

"I'd like to know what you would like to tell me, Pearl. Your purpose here, with me, is to work through anything you feel you may need help with."

"How do I look to you?"

"Do you want me to answer?"

Pearl's eyes narrowed.

"Since you asked. Your hair appears to have not been washed in some time. The tangles in it indicate your grooming skills have fallen to the wayside a bit. I am not sure when you last brushed it, but my guess is it wasn't this morning. Your clothes are unkempt and fairly baggy, so I would guess you have lost a good amount of weight. Diet hasn't been agreeing with you?"

Pearl said nothing.

"You mentioned having trouble sleeping. The circles under your eyes and the texture of your skin relay that sleep is not much of an issue. In fact, they tell me the opposite—that you get entirely too much sleep. Am I far off?"

No. I'll give you that one, Doc.

"Tell me how things have been going. Remember, this is a safe place. You can say what you want here."

Pearl's fingers stopped wrestling with each other and slowly began forming tight fists. Pearl began breathing heavily. Dr. Lenowitz observed this behavior but said nothing.

"You're right. I haven't showered in days. Not since I went hiking last week. I don't have the energy for it. I barely have enough energy to cry anymore, which I've done an awful lot. Yes, I sleep too much but sleeping helps me remember—Remember her, remember us, remember my life when it was good. Not like it is now; all messed up. I don't expect you to understand. Nobody understands."

"Do you feel like you're forgetting the life you had with her?"

"How can I? My whole life has been about the connection we had. I feel her presence constantly, even though she isn't here. But I don't want to forget the life we shared. Except for *that* night."

"Why do you want to forget *that* night?"

"One guess."

"Because Jade died?"

The words sliced across Pearl's throat, emotionally bleeding her from the statement as she gasped for words of rebuttal but could not manage to find any. She couldn't help but cry. Her hands unclenched in her lap and rescued her tears.

"Pearl?"

"What do you want?"

"To help. How can I help?"

"Got a time machine?"

"No, but I can do my best to help you in the present. Not enough sleep isn't really the issue, is it?"

"No. I sleep *too* much. What I really need is to sleep without dreaming."

After that, Pearl retreated and did not interact any further. The two sat for the remainder of the session in silence. Pearl didn't look up. She just studied her hands that seemed to be twitching relentlessly.

Dr. Lenowitz confirmed that the session had come to an end. As Pearl rose from her chair and headed for the door, they scheduled her next session. Just as Pearl grabbed the handle of the door to leave, Dr. Lenowitz stopped her from turning the knob and handed her the prescription. “It will help you sleep.”

Pearl nodded her head in agreement, took the prescription, and headed out the door.

She arrived at Marlene’s car and climbed in, winded and tired. She studied the words written on Dr. Lenowitz’s prescription pad.

Maybe this will be my cure.

“What are you hungry for today, sweetie? How about some ice cream? My treat.” Marlene said.

“Sure.”

Marlene smiled at Pearl’s response. For a moment, she had her daughter back—her daughter, who loved going for ice cream and chatting up a storm about her day. Looking at the passenger seat, a memory of the old Pearl came back to her. *Back to the old Pearl.*

NINE

Jade and Ezekiel strolled down the hall to Group. Jade shared stories of growing up in a large Hispanic and Irish family. She spoke of her summer vacations at Lost Lake Campground and her family visits to Boston. She shared how she fell in love with Boston and had planned to play lacrosse there. Ezekiel shared his experience of life in California, which blended his passion for snowboarding and baseball.

Two new members joined today, and three moved on.

"Hi, everyone, my name is Emerick," the newest member of the group greeted. He recently succumbed to cystic fibrosis at sixteen. His chipper demeanor infected the group as he smiled through his introduction.

I've never seen someone so happy in here. It's awesome.

He spoke about his experience with CF and how he

surpassed his doctors' prediction of not reaching age eight. He flashed a large smile as he spoke to the group, pulling them in with intrigue and wonder.

"Your demeanor is shocking," Jason expressed.

Emerick glanced over and, with the largest of smiles, said, "Jason, when you pass your death age by nine years, it's considered a victory."

Jason's eyebrows raised as he nodded.

That's one way to put it. He makes a good point.

"I'm sixteen. You were how old? Seventeen? Eighteen?" Emerick asked.

"Fourteen," Jason responded.

"Wow, kudos to you. You look way older than fourteen," Emerick said. Jason smiled. "We all look at it like, 'Oh my, I died young.' But why aren't we looking at it as 'I lived long?' It's not like we get stamped when we are born and told, 'See you back here at eighty-two.' Tomorrow is never promised, and none of us are guaranteed to live to eighty, or sixty, or even thirty-five. So, the fact we made it past birth should be celebrated because some people don't even make it that far. You know what I mean?"

Jason glanced to the side, smothering his upper lip with his bottom one.

"You know?" Emerick asked.

"Yes, I know what you mean," Yousef chimed in—

another new member of the group. He stood up from his chair and straightened his attire in preparation for his greeting. “I come by way of a birth defect, which should have only permitted me to live up to five years. I managed to make it to sixteen. I remember my parents being very sad that I had to leave, but it calmed them when they were reminded that I made it longer than expected.”

“I never thought about this the way you two are explaining it. It’s very insightful. Thank you,” Jade said.

“No problem. I hope it helps you move along,” Yousef said.

“It helps.” *I still need to know how I died.*

Jade lowered her head, closed her eyes, and placed her index finger on her right temple, massaging it in a circular motion. She opened her eyes to see Ezekiel and the rest of the group staring at her with curious eyes.

Did I grunt out loud? She looked to Ezekiel wide-eyed, lips tucked in, then lipped the words, “I was drunk” to him.

“Are you okay, Jade?” Chase interrupted.

She quickly gathered herself. *Say something witty. Throw off the vibe you’re getting*. She breathed deeply and focused on Chase. *Or just tell the truth.* “I was drunk.”

“Drunk?”

“Yes. The night I died, I was drunk.”

"Ah. It's happening," Chase said. "You are starting to remember now. This means you are making progress."

Jade glanced at Ezekiel and noticed his large smile. He raised his index finger and mouthed the words, "One step closer." *One step closer to the freedom of knowing.* Jade couldn't wait to continue getting one step closer. Peace.

One piece of the puzzle is in place. Man, this feels good.

"How does it feel? Now the pieces are starting to come together?" Chase asked.

"I don't feel as lame anymore," Jade responded, causing a chuckle among the group members.

"Would you like to share more?"

"Like what?"

"Being drunk. Did it happen often?"

"I'm a teenager, so going to parties was the norm. I wouldn't say drunkenness happened often, though."

"Who would you normally party with?"

"My sister. We hung out together. We did a lot with each other."

"Like what?"

The spring pep rally popped into Jade's head. She shared the story of the senior class skit. Jade had played the role of a quirky detective who had to solve the mystery of the missing prom theme. She ran out wearing a pink tutu and Hawaiian shirt, delivering a monologue about clues that lower classmen had collected throughout the week. Pearl had played the role of the villain and, throughout the skit, had followed Jade around without her knowing.

Jade became animated in her description, tweaking her face to speak like her character, and she jumped from her seat, performing outlandish maneuvers. The group laughed at her antics and clapped upon conclusion.

"Thank you, thank you," Jade said, bowing in acceptance of the applause.

Her eyes expanded as she puffed out her cheeks. She glanced over at Chase and said, "We were together. Pearl and I."

"Good. More progress. I'm so proud of you."

……

Jade's natural high continued following Group as she met with Adelaide.

"You seem like you're in a good mood today," Adelaide said.

"I am. I remembered something about the night I died."

"Oh, you did now. Let's hear it." Her curiosity was clearly stirring.

"Not much, but I do remember that I was drunk."

"Hmm, interesting. Anything else pop in your head from that night?"

"Pearl and I were together."

"Good. Anything else?"

Jade sat down in the chair next to the door. She closed her eyes and plugged her ears with her fingers. Adelaide nudged her on the shoulder, "You okay?"

Jade appeared defeated. "Nothing, I got nothing. I don't get it. Why is it so hard for me to remember?" *I feel like such a failure at this.*

Adelaide sighed. "Darling, sometimes memories can be suppressed because you are afraid of what will be brought up with them. Sometimes that fear can be hard to deal with. Does this make sense?"

"I guess it does. I only drank at parties, so if I remember being drunk, I must have been at a party."

"You are starting to remember now. Who knows how much longer it will take. But you are making progress. Be patient with it, okay?"

"You got it," Jade responded, as she mimicked a gun motion with her two hands, pretending to shoot at Adelaide while simultaneously winking her left eye and clicking her tongue.

……

Jade met up with Ezekiel for their usual post-Group consult. Ezekiel embraced Jade with a hug so strong that she could feel her heartbeat in her brain. Ezekiel seemed different.

His usual banter about high school shows he engulfed himself in—particularly theories of his favorite show about zombies that hunt humans—had been replaced with silence. Ezekiel began to walk in a new direction, and Jade followed along, unaware of where they were heading.

I hope he is okay.

"I died in a car accident," Ezekiel shared suddenly.

Whoa, I didn't expect that. "This is the first time you are sharing your story with me."

"I know." He breathed deeply. "It was Saturday night. The usual party night. I got into an argument with my parents because they didn't want me driving to a big party in a snowstorm. The snow had made the roads slick that day, which made car wrecks much more likely. I understand now why they didn't want me to go. But, that night, I was pissed off because it was the primo party of the year and I'd have been damned if I missed it, you know?"

Jade nodded.

"So, the plan went as such," Ezekiel continued. "When the folks fell asleep, my buddy would pick me up, and we'd head to the party—no big deal. I would be home before they woke up, and all would be well. Naturally, if I had known then what I know now, I would have stayed home.

So, we make it to the party. I remember feeling like

a ninja because my mom and dad had no idea that I left. We partied for a good few hours and then headed home. Easy-peasy, right? We hopped back into my buddy's car and were making good time. We were only ten minutes away. Until that, damn... I don't even know what… came across the road at 2:00 A.M. The car swerved to the right, then back to the left, fishtailed, and the next thing we knew, we were heading sideways at a tree off the bank. Wrapped the car right around it."

How horrible.

"It all happened so fast. If I had just listened to my parents, I wouldn't be in this situation right now. Just like that," Ezekiel snapped his fingers. Jade blinked rapidly at the sound.

"I'm sorry that happened to you."

"Completely avoidable. My parents were sound asleep when they got a call from the cops saying I died from a car wreck. You can imagine their shock because they thought I was asleep in my room the whole time. My decision to party clearly outweighed the possibility that my parents could end their night identifying me in the morgue. When I first arrived here, I couldn't handle that. My biggest task was to work through my guilt—especially because of how devastated my mom was. She thought she had failed as a mother.

You know what it's like doing a visit and not being able to communicate?"

I know all too well.

Ezekiel shook his head. "Of course, you do. My first visit went badly. I wanted to apologize to my parents and let them know they were great parents, but I couldn't. I think waiting for them to release their guilt became a key component for me.

So, after your second visit, you get to keep your amulet and see your family in it whenever you want. That ability usually makes for a much better third visit."

"Really?" Jade said. Her eyes lit up with excitement.

"It's a great tool for healing. I watched every time my parents went to grief counseling. Seeing them get better helped me get better."

"So, is that why you're still here?"

"Partially. I needed to see them heal, but I also wanted to see you heal."

"Me?"

"Yes, you silly. We connected so well when you first got here, but you were blocked. I stalled my own progress to stay and see you heal, but I'm all better now, and can no longer stay."

All better? Where is he going with this?

Ezekiel guided Jade's arm under his as they ventured to an unfamiliar part of the grounds. The path, which was sprinkled with roses, opened up to a large field of grass with a single wooden bench sitting twenty feet from a large ivy wall. The two sat on the bench as thick silence filled the air. Jade studied the ivy.

What does that ivy hold? It's so massive.

"You look confused."

"A little."

"This is where we go."

"For what?"

"When we move on."

"Where does it take you?"

"I'm assuming it's different for everyone."

"That makes sense."

"It's where I will be going."

"Going?"

"Yes. I am ready. I have been ready. I put off moving on as long as I could, but I can't stay anymore. I have no more time. I've done my work. My heart sings, knowing you are starting to remember. That puts you one step closer to your own healing."

Ezekiel placed his palm on Jade's cheek and sighed. "I can't stay. I must leave. Now."

No. He can't. Not now.

She tilted her head into Ezekiel's palm and moistened his skin with her tears. She said nothing, but Ezekiel knew.

"Hey, look at me. This isn't goodbye. It's a 'see you in a bit.' I love you, Jade. Remember that, please. You're my person."

His person?

Jade said nothing. The pain shattered her speech as she stood there crying, paralyzed. He embraced her once more as she dug her head into his chest. "I know. I know," he said as he stroked her hair and continued rubbing her back. For a second, the world disappeared, and they were the only two present, lost in the moment. But in that same moment, they were also found—because they had found each other.

This isn't happening right now.

Ezekiel wiped the tears from her cheek with his thumb, staring intently in her eyes. In a somber voice, he said, "I have to go."

Jade nodded her head in agreement. Ezekiel loosened his grip and took a step back. He smiled at her and continued to take steps back as the ivy wall became illuminated, presenting a bright vertical rectangle in front of it. Jade held her hand up, shielding her eyes from the brightness.

"Hey," Ezekiel said. "Soon?"

Jade smiled, "Soon."

She stood paralyzed as the distance between them increased. For a moment, nothing made sense—not what had happened to Ezekiel, not why he had to leave—it made no sense at all. She held her hand to her chest as her breathing became erratic. A tingling sensation vibrated through her body as she released a heavy sigh, realizing she had feelings beyond friendship for him.

“Wait!” She yelled as she sprinted towards the ivy wall, her heart pounding as words in her throat attempted to escape. The wall seemed a mile away. Finally, her hands hit the ivy and halted her in place. Staring at the dull green leaves, she desperately looked for Ezekiel. But he was nowhere in sight. The gut-wrenching feeling intensified as she mustered the only words she could, “I love you too, Zeek.”

She was alone.

TEN

"Who's ready to watch some football?" Pearl hollered as she bounced down the stairs to meet her family, her curls springing with every skip. Marlene and Jeff were in shock to see their daughter in such good spirits. Pearl appeared better after taking the medication Dr. Lenowitz prescribed, but they could never have imagined her being this happy—her hair washed, makeup done, an increase in appetite. The family traveled to watch Jamie play their league rivals at the University of Oregon. Sander joined them for the outing. They sat in the back of the SUV, chit-chatting and laughing, provoking a slap or two from Andrew, followed by a "sshhhh."

Shoosh me. I don't care. It's worth it. He makes me happy. I'm indebted to him for helping me.

The family sat on the fifty-yard line, five rows back. The

atmosphere of the game, the band's fight song, the cheerleaders, and the musical dance sessions between outings put Pearl in a good place. Sander could see her happiness as he gave her a big squeeze. "I'm glad you're having fun."

Pearl returned Sander's gesture with a kiss on the cheek. Sander released his grip on Pearl and continued to smile as he diverted her attention to the game.

Odd. Why didn't he kiss me back? Pearl didn't know how to take Sander's behavior, so she cracked a smile and attempted to keep her focus on the game. She made her way to the concession stand at half-time. *I guess my appetite made its way back.*

The concession line oozed with Ducks and Cardinal fans—a mix of green and dark red flowing through the halls of the stadium. Pearl stood patiently in line, receiving play-by-play messages from Sander about the half-time show when a voice she recognized whispered behind her.

"Please, don't walk away from me."

Henry. Not today, not here. Pearl didn't bother turning around. She continued her phone texts with Sander, ignoring the sounds from Henry's mouth.

"I thought I gave her the upper. I didn't know the labels were wrong. Please, forgive me."

Shut up.

"I haven't been able to sleep since this happened. I made

a mistake, and I'm very sorry."

'Sorry' won't bring her back. Her knuckles reddened by the grip on her phone as she picked it up to text.

"I know this put a rift in our relationship, and as hard as it is for me, I'm coming to terms with the fact that we are no longer friends. But I need your forgiveness, Pearl."

Pearl halted texting. She wanted to leave the line. She lowered her phone to her side and slowly rotated to face Henry. His eyes were sorrowful and bloodshot.

"In an attempt to not make a scene, I will keep this short. You should feel bad. You gave drugs to someone who had never tried them before. You were careless with your product and my sister paid her life for it. You deserve to never receive forgiveness for your actions, but you are the one who must live with your decisions for the rest of your life, not me. I must live without my sister, which, to me, is much worse. No, we are no longer friends. Not even acquaintances anymore, and that will never change. I will, however, say my sister is… was… a big girl and could have made her own decisions. She paid her life for it and will never get it back. I will say this to you in my final breath in your direction. I forgive you for your lack of judgement, costing my sister her life."

Sander arrived and placed his hand on Pearl's shoulder, startling her and causing the phone to plummet to the ground.

"Everything okay here?" Sander asked.

"Fine," Pearl responded, her eyes still fixed on Henry. *Thank goodness you are here.*

Henry instinctively picked up the phone and wiped off the screen that had collected debris from the fall. He glanced at the phone to a text conversation between Pearl and Sander:

PEARL: HENRY. 911.

SANDER: ON MY WAY.

Pearl: OK.

"Guess I deserve that," Henry said, handing Pearl the phone. "Goodbye, Pearl." He made his way through the crowd, becoming engulfed in the sea of green and red.

Her eyes misted. *Goodbye, my friend. Chapter closed.* His actions angered her, and she felt betrayed by Henry for what had happened to Jade. *I would never have imagined in a million lifetimes that someone so close to me would do such a thing*. For a moment, Pearl wanted to reach out and apologize to him, but she now lacked the energy to chase him down. *You make me sad. Sad to see you go, sad that you did this.*

"It'll be okay. You'll see," Sander said.

He's not your friend. You can't even fathom understanding this. The nerve.

Pearl blinked her eyes rapidly to restart her thought process. "What do you want to eat?" She asked Sander with a smile on her face.

"What?"

"Eat. Food. What would you like?"

Sander studied Pearl. To avoid dwelling on the subject, he responded, "Um, I'll have a hot dog."

"Sweet." Pearl glanced at the concession worker. "Two hot dogs, please."

……

Pearl sat in her room, pondering her relationship with Sander. She had feelings for him but didn't know how to decipher them. *Around him, I'm happy, free, diverted from my situation. Not around him, the sadness is overwhelming.* She pulled out her phone and touched the green and white thought bubble:

PEARL: HEY.

SANDER: WHAT'S UP?

PEARL: CHILLING. WHATCHA DOING?

SANDER: RIGHT NOW? TAMING COBRAS. YOU?

PEARL: PERFORMING A HIGH-WIRE ACT AS WE SPEAK.

SANDER: LOOK AT YOU, MULTI-TASKING.

PEARL: Come over.

SANDER: Can't.

PEARL: Why not?

SANDER: Busy right now.

PEARL: I need you.

SANDER: What's wrong?

PEARL: Not feeling good.

SANDER: Henry on your mind?

PEARL: Sure. I wanted to die when I saw him.

SANDER: Don't say that.

PEARL: It brought back stuff. Both good and bad. I can't stand that I feel this way. Makes me want to leave here.

SANDER: You don't mean that.

PEARL: Tempting.

SANDER: You need to stay here. Who else am I going to hang out with?

PEARL: Whatevs. Why?

SANDER: Because I care about

you

and what happens to you.

There it is. He cares for me. I want to tell him I like him and hope my feelings are reciprocated.

PEARL: Can I tell you something?

SANDER: Sure, sweetie. What's up?

Pearl stalled. *What if he rejects me?* Sharing her feelings seemed a lot better than executing the task. *Would I make a fool out of myself by confessing my love for him? What if he thinks I'm a screwed up little girl who doesn't know what she wants?*

PEARL: Thanks for today. You

were my knight in shining armor.

SANDER: I don't know about

knight status.

PEARL: Fine. Thank you for

today, peasant.

SANDER: Dork. Fine, I'll take

it.

You have a good evening, your

majesty.

"Mom?" Pearl's voice echoed through the house.

Marlene rushed up to her room. "Yes, dear?"

“Let’s go to a movie.”

“Oh, okay. What do you want to see?”

“There’s a romantic comedy about a girl who meets a guy from out of town and gets swept off her feet. How does that one sound?”

“Oh, you mean *Strange Bliss*?”

“Yep, that’s the one.”

“OK, let me grab my purse, and then we’ll head out, good?”

As Marlene went to retrieve her purse, Pearl pondered over the movie. *Maybe the movie can give me some idea of how to talk to Sander and tell him how I feel.*

The movie didn’t surprise Pearl. Stranger meets girl, sweeps her off her feet, they fall in love, but he ends up leaving. Girl falls for his friend, and they live happily ever after. She studied what the characters said, and how the lead actress confessed her love. She knew they were acting, but, in real life, the plan could work.

What if he does leave? The idea sank in her chest and weighed heavily on her gut. “I don’t think I could deal with my true love leaving in those circumstances,” Pearl said, munching on the last of the popcorn as they exited the theatre.

“I know. It must have been very hard for her. I met your father when we were young, and we have been together for a long time. The thought of him not being around gives me a sick feeling."

"I kind of feel that way about Sander," Pearl said.

"Oh, you do?"

Here we go. Fifty questions.

"I get this feeling when I'm around him. He makes me feel safe. As though he popped up in Group one day, poof. He doesn't share a whole lot of his story in Group. Is that weird?"

"Not at all. Some people are less inclined to be open about their experiences. It may take him more time. But don't pry too much, honey. It may push him away."

"Ugh. Don't push. Don't stay away. The fine line is ridiculous. What are we to do?"

"Be patient and let it happen organically."

"You're such a hippie, Mom."

"I did go to Berkeley."

The two chuckled.

They trudged through the front door after 10:30 P.M. Marlene stumbled up the stairs for some much-needed sleep. Pearl opened her door and paused, looking at her mother, who stood in her bedroom doorway, releasing her feet from the constraints of her ballet flats.

"Mom."

Marlene paused and turned her head around to Pearl.

"Yes, dear?"

"I enjoyed tonight. Thanks."

She couldn't contain her happiness. "You're very welcome, my dear. Get some sleep, okay? Want to do something tomorrow?"

"Maybe."

"Okay. Let me know."

"Okay. Goodnight."

"Night."

Pearl fell onto her bed and activated the green and white comment icon on her phone.

PEARL: I WATCHED A MOVIE TODAY ABOUT A STRANGER WHO CAME INTO THIS GIRL'S LIFE AND CHANGED IT FOREVER. IT REMINDED ME OF YOU.

SANDER: I HOPE IT ENDED WELL, LOL.

PEARL: HE ENDED UP LEAVING, AND IT DEVASTATED HER.

SANDER: DOESN'T SOUND GOOD AT ALL. REMINDS YOU OF ME?

PEARL: THE GOOD PARTS DO. SHE

ENDS

UP HAPPY.

SANDER: WHEW. WHAT A RELIEF

TO

HEAR.

PEARL: THANK YOU FOR COMING

INTO

MY LIFE.

SANDER: AW, YOU'RE WELCOME,

MY

DEAR. IT HAS BEEN AN ABSOLUTE

PLEASURE.

PEARL: I HOPE YOU STICK AROUND

FOR

A WHILE.

SANDER: I'LL STICK AROUND AS

LONG

AS I CAN.

What the hell does that mean? He did it again. No return of affection. Does he not like me that way? Should I say something to him?

PEARL: SANDER? ONE LAST THING.

SANDER: ANYTHING YOUR MAJESTY.

Her thumbs halted to formulate the words. *What if I ruin everything?*

PEARL: LET'S GET SOME TEA TOMORROW. YEAH?

SANDER: SOUNDS LIKE A PLAN.

PEARL: GREAT. SEE YOU TOMORROW, PEASANT.

Crisis averted for now. I'll just leave it be and see how it goes... if it goes anywhere at all. I hope it does.

ELEVEN

"I'm not sure how I feel knowing that my daily life will be different without Ezekiel," Jade said.

"My guess is it will be a little different. You two did spend quite a bit of time together. Yes?" Adelaide said.

"I suppose. I considered him a close friend until…"

"Until what?"

Jade stood quietly.

"Jade? Don't leave me hanging like that."

"Ugh. Okay. Before he left, he told me he loved me. He told me I'm his person. When he walked into the ivy, I realized I loved him too."

"Aw. That's very sweet…"

"But, he disappeared before I could tell him."

"Oh. Are you sure he didn't hear you?"

"Completely. He was clear out of sight and the light no longer illuminated the wall."

"Oh, Jade. That must have been tough for you. How are you doing now?"

"It literally just happened, so I'm still absorbing it. I've never used the word 'love' with someone before. Except for my family."

"Love is a tricky thing, darling. How is Group going?"

"I feel great, and I'm making good progress. I'm feeling very focused."

"That's amazing. It sounds like you've had an eventful day. Why don't you go and get some rest?"

"Good idea. Thanks for everything."

"It's been my pleasure."

Once in her room, Jade noticed a lavender envelope that had been placed on her pillow. *I wonder what's inside?* She picked it up and unfolded the parchment inside. She could immediately tell that Ezekiel had written it, so she sat down and began reading.

My dearest Jade,

By the time you read this letter, I will be gone. I can't put into words what our time has meant to me. I felt like I would spend eternity being miserable until you came along. You are such a beautiful person inside and out. I cannot wait until the next time I see you. Be prepared for the biggest hug. I'll miss you... fiercely.

Zeek

The warming sensation returned to her chest, then traveled in all directions through her limbs and up to her head. Her eyes misted as she smiled, thinking about the words Ezekiel had left her. She sat on her bed, staring, crying, smiling. *What am I going to do next?* Then it hit her. One word struck Jade's brain hard—recovery. Jade found herself saying, "I need to recover. I need this for me and for Pearl."

She jumped up from her bed and knew what she had to do. Swinging the door open, she sped down the hall to Adelaide's office. She formulated her plan in her head while she rushed down the hall. *I'll go to her group and hopefully get some information then. Anything will help. I must stay focused. Must stay focused.*

Jade approached Adelaide's office and noticed the door had been shut. *Hmm, the door is always open this time of day. How strange*. Curiosity got the best of her as she leaned in and pressed her ear against the door, listening to the unfolding conversation.

"I can't believe you are telling me this. How could this happen?" Jade heard Adelaide say.

"It just happened," another voice said. It was a male

voice, one Jade didn't recognize.

"Okay, let's think here. Is there any way to remedy this?"

"I'm not sure. The signs are there. She doesn't seem to be making progress."

"What indicators do you have of this?"

"Listening to what she says and how she acts. She goes up and down."

"How could you let it get to this? You know this will be reported. It's highly unprofessional of you."

"I know, I'm sorry. This has never happened to me."

"I know. I'm well aware of your record. This poses quite a dilemma."

Who were they discussing? Me? She pressed her ear harder against the door.

"I know. I didn't expect this to happen," the male voice continued.

"Are you sure it is genuine?"

"I'm positive. Look at the messages."

I wonder who they are talking about.

"I will look into this. You keep doing what you do best, okay?"

"I think my participation has become detrimental to the overall process. It won't end well when I leave."

"Do the best you can. I have faith in you."

"Fine. I will try to prepare her. I'll say I'm moving out of state or something. Geez, Adelaide, this sucks. I kind of like her. I know it's against the rules, but still."

"You know Guardian Energies can't be with the living."

"Yes, I know. It's my luck. I better head out. It's Game Night with the family. See you later. I'll report any progress back to you."

Crap. Jade quickly took a step back and raised her hand into a knocking position.

The door opened. Adelaide's visitor stood there, wide-eyed, staring at Jade. She extended her hand.

"Hi. My name is Jade. Are you new here? Sorry, I didn't know Adelaide had a meeting."

The visitor said nothing. He glanced at Adelaide, who nodded for him to respond. He extended his hand out to meet Jade's and shook it.

"Hi Jade, I'm Sander. Pleasure to meet you."

"Sander is a crisis team member, Jade. He gets sent to handle situations for people who need a little extra care," Adelaide said.

"Yes. Monopoly tonight with the family. Should be fun," Sander said.

"The top hat is the lucky piece. FYI," Jade said.

"Oh, that piece is off-limits," Sander said.

Jade tilted her head to the side and narrowed her eyes for a second. *Off-limits?*

Sander abruptly adjusted the conversation. “I have to go, or else I’ll be late. Pleasure meeting you, Jade.”

“Have fun.”

Sander exited the room and made haste down the corridor. He then took a left at the end of the hall.

“I wonder what family he’s visiting. I hope it all works out.”

“In the end, I’m sure it will,” Adelaide said.

Jade took her spot in the chair by the desk.

“What brings you by? Long time no see.”

“Recovery. I’m ready to keep going, and I have a plan to get there.”

“Okay, what are you suggesting?”

“I would like to take my second visit. I need my second visit. I think it will help me. I’ve come quite a way since my first visit, and I’m ready to do this.”

“Does this have anything to do with Ezekiel?”

Seriously? “I have come to the realization that I need to do this for me. Griping about my situation didn’t make things better. The peace on Ezekiel’s face when he moved on is something I want to feel. I need peace and finding out what happened to me will help me get there.”

"Okay. We can schedule it. Any day you're interested in?"

"How is next Saturday during Group? If she shares anything, it will be there."

"You sure? If you say yes, I'll pencil that date in for you,"

"Very sure."

Adelaide looked down at her desk planner and circled the following Saturday. She opened the leather-bound book and flipped forward to September 23rd and wrote, "Jade, 10:00 A.M. Second visit." Adelaide smiled at Jade. "Okay, we are good to go."

Jade felt relieved, knowing that she just took the next step in recovery. Seeing her sister would be a bonus. As she walked back to her bedroom to write in her journal, she started feeling guilty about her lack of interest in seeing the rest of her family. *I don't have any quarrels with my family, but why am I not excited to see them?*

She arrived at her room and immediately opened her journal. She wrote about saying goodbye to Ezekiel, arranging her second visit, and meeting a Guardian Energy. She wrote about her upcoming visit and her excitement to see Pearl again, creating scripted artistry on the paper as she wrote.

I'm confused as to why I'm not itching to see my brothers and parents... she wrote. *It's not like I had beef with any of them. There were never any issues with them before I died...* Jade paused. *No beef. No issues. We weren't on bad terms. Could that be why I am not itching to see them? Because I don't have unfinished business?*

She quickly jotted down on a separate piece of paper, *Talk to Adelaide about unfinished business.*

Jade sifted through past journal entries. Her transformation since arriving stared at her on the lined paper. While she contemplated losing her life, Ezekiel, and her memory, she came to a sobering realization about all she had lost since her arrival. The pain gave her a knot in her stomach. She dropped the pen she was holding and placed her palm on her abdomen as if holding in her insides so they wouldn't fall out. But they stayed. The pain increased with every second until Jade couldn't take the sensation anymore. She curled up into the fetal position on her bed and wrapped her arms around her knees, sobbing. *Stop crying, you'll see him soon.* Unable to process her physical condition, she continued her emotional release. *I've never felt this way before. Why is someone making me cry this much?* She knew why but couldn't explain it. She cried until her whimpers turned into a low moan—then fell asleep.

TWELVE

Pearl and Sander took their designated game pieces—the race car and boot—for Game Night like they did the past few weeks. The top hat sat off the game board, having lost its player and not allowed to play since. "Jade always played with the top hat," Pearl had informed Sander the first time he joined the game. Pearl often invited Sander to family Game Night on Sundays after dinner. But this night felt different. Sander remained quiet during set up.

"You okay?" Pearl asked.

"I'm fine. Just tired."

"Oh, okay. Let me know if you need anything. Such as a butt-whooping."

"Right. I'm taking you down tonight, girly."

Though he had been trained to not fall for assigned

clients, Sander couldn't help but smile at Pearl when she glanced at him from across the coffee table. Her face was fresh, sans makeup, and her onyx hair was up in a messy bun. Her smile reflected her happiness.

"I'll start it off," Pearl declared. She seemed antsy to get the game going. Marlene and Jeff didn't object to their daughter going first. The family members took their positions around the coffee table. They gathered pillows and sat on their knees to prepare. Sander had previously been warned that Game Night could get intense, which is why they played in the living room instead of on the kitchen table. Jeff and Marlene sat next to each other, Andrew sat across from them, and Sander and Pearl sat across from each other.

Sander watched Pearl and Andrew bicker over who would own the most property by the end of the game. Pearl purchased Baltic on the first try, Andrew followed up by capturing Vermont and Connecticut. Marlene and Jeff declined to purchase any property. Instead, they enjoyed the view of their children having fun playing the game. Sander got sent to jail three times, which resulted in some snide remarks from Pearl about him being a rebel. The game continued for a few hours—the players buying, selling, paying rents, passing go, and collecting 200 dollars.

"I can't wait for you to land on Park Place so I can ream your earnings," Pearl said.

"Yeah right, punk," Andrew said.

Jokes were made, and everyone was smiling. For the first time in a while, the family appeared to be a unit.

Andrew picked up his game piece and began counting spaces. One, two, three…as if the play was cast in slow motion. He let out a loud sigh as his piece landed on the dreaded Park Place. He glanced over at Pearl as she rubbed her hands together with the most malicious of looks.

"Mwahaha, I'll get you my pretty, and all your money, too," she laughed. Andrew grimaced, having been defeated by his sister. "Don't mess with the Pearlinator in Monopoly, young man, or you… will… lose."

"Haha, 'Pearlinator.' How original, sis. I'll let you have this one, but I'll get you next time. No dance like usual?"

Pearl's expression relaxed as she avoided her brother's question.

"Dance? What dance? Let's see some moves," Sander requested.

Please no.

"It's silly. I used to do this line dance when I landed a high rent."

"It's hilarious. Jade would do this bit with her top hat like a showgirl," Marlene said.

Pearl's eyes drifted away and onto the game board.

……

"Bada bada bada. I've got your money, baby. All your money, baby. You're so broke. It's no joke," Jade sang as she tipped her top hat piece forward off her head then put it back on as Pearl landed on Park Place. Park Place was usually owned by one of the two girls, and their songs were entertainment when others landed on their property.

Pearl jumped up to join in the fun, stomping her right foot and clapping her hands in rhythmic half-time. She interluded, "Spin your property round and round, throw your landlord to the ground, pick her up by the hair, then pull down her underwear."

Marlene and Jeff roared with laughter as their daughters continued song-battling each other.

"Start spreading the dough, cause now you live on my row."

"Hot dawg, partner!"

There was jumping, kicking, jazz hands, laughter-induced stomach pains, and monopoly.

……

"Show him, Pearl," Andrew said.

Pearl bit her inner cheek as she looked up and narrowed her left eye, staring at Andrew.

"Come on. Sander would love to see it."

"I would have to agree with Andrew. I'd love to see this

routine of yours."

Why is this dance so important to you?

Pearl's attention refocused on the top hat. It sat there alone, asking to be used, to be played.

"Fine," Pearl said. She grabbed the hat and placed it gently on her head as she imitated Jade's routine of kickball changes and shuffles. In her excited state, she flung her arms out in a "tada" motion, her gesture catapulting the top hat into the air. Pearl immediately panicked when she heard the game piece ping off into the distance.

"The top hat!" Pearl gasped as she jumped up and frantically began searching for it. Her parents offered to help find the piece, but Pearl ignored their offer and continued combing the carpet and furniture in search of the piece.

"How far could it have gone?" Pearl said, her voice cracking.

Marlene took a step towards her but was stopped by Jeff. "Let her look on her own, sweetie. She will find it."

Pearl progressed to the kitchen, scouring the baseboards until a small glimpse of the kitchen light, pierced her eye with a sudden flash, revealing a small metal figurine under the counter. She stumbled, her feet behind pace of her hands, and grabbed the piece to examine and confirm that it was the top hat. Pearl sat on the kitchen floor, cupping the game piece in her hands, licking her thumb to clean the top. Sander made his way to Pearl to comfort her, but Andrew's hand stopped him.

"Maybe not, bro. We should let her handle this one." Sander tapped his palm on Andrew's hand in reassurance, but Andrew held firm and shook his head resolutely. Sander succumbed to Andrew's request and sat down on the couch.

Pearl curled up on the kitchen floor, talking to herself. Inaudible to the family, she comforted the hat, providing it with a support speech.

"I'm sorry, Jade. I won't ever lose you again. I'm sorry about being careless. I won't lose you again." Tears saturated her face as she cradled the game piece. Jeff slowly lowered himself in front of her and reached his hands out.

"Hey," he whispered. "You found it." He motioned his hands to hers, but she shuddered. "It's okay. You are doing a great job taking care of it."

Pearl did not reply. She sat studying the top hat, examining it for injury. She exhaled deeply and glanced up at Jeff, "I almost lost her, Dad. Again. How could I be so reckless?"

Jeff offered Pearl the only piece of advice he could think to give. Tightening his hands around hers, gently squeezing her hands around the game piece, he looked Pearl in the eyes and whispered, "Hey, you didn't lose her. She's still here, and always will be," as he tapped Pearl's chest with his index finger.

He has no idea. None at all. Pearl sat there in a daze, repeating her chant, "I almost lost her. I almost lost her."

Jeff helplessly glanced at Marlene, who sat there staring, waiting to hear a prognosis. He asked, "Mind if I take her upstairs?" Marlene held her hands together against her lips and nodded.

Jeff leaned into Pearl and placed his forehead against hers. "Hey, look at me," he whispered. She looked up and made eye contact. He smiled and continued, "Let's go put this somewhere safe, okay? How does that sound?"

Pearl nodded, "Okay, Dad."

"Good. Alright, sweetie, I'm going to need your help. Wrap your arms around my neck so I can pick you up."

Pearl obliged. She placed the game piece in her right hand and gripped it tightly as she wrapped her arms around Jeff's neck. In one swoop, he lifted Pearl from the floor.

"I'll get her up and settled and will make sure she is okay," Jeff said.

"I'm going to join you," Marlene said. She stroked Pearl's head, parting her hair from her face, exposing her swollen eyes. Jeff agreed with a short nod, his chin quivering.

"We'll be right back," Marlene said to Sander.

"Can I do anything to help?" Sander asked.

"We will let you know. Thank you for being here, Sander.

I'm sure she'll want to see you when she comes around."

Jeff carried a limp and exhausted Pearl up the stairs to her room.

"And just like that…" Andrew said.

Sander gave him a glance of disapproval.

"What? It's always two steps forward, four steps back with her."

"That's not very kind, Andrew."

"This isn't a kind situation, Sander."

Jeff and Marlene returned from upstairs, collapsing on the couch. Marlene buried her head in Jeff's chest and began sobbing.

"Right when we had her, we lost her again. How much longer will this go on? I'm afraid one day she won't…"

"Won't what?" Jeff asked, tilting Marlene's chin away from his chest.

Marlene paused, her eyes staring down the game, her shoulders slouched in defeat. "Won't want to stay."

"Don't say that, dear."

"I can't hear this right now," Andrew said, backing away from his parents. "I can't believe you're even thinking about her..."

"I'm sorry. I'm sorry. I just… what has happened to our family?" Marlene asked.

"We've experienced a tragedy, but are working through it the best we can. We need to stay patient and together on this. It won't happen overnight, but we need to stay strong for our kids," Jeff said.

"But what about us? We lost a child and are losing another one. She barely eats, only has fleeting moments of happiness that don't last long, and when Sander is not around her, she is a cloud of sadness," Marlene said.

Jeff grabbed Andrew, pulled him to the couch, and took Marlene into his arms, hugging them both.

Sander sat in his chair, frustrated he couldn't snap his fingers to make it all better. He experienced this before, but never with people he had an emotional connection with.

"May I go see her now?"

Marlene nodded.

……

Sander sat at Pearl's desk as she slept. He studied the photos of her and Jade that were pinned onto the corkboard. *Sixteenth birthday party. Eighth grade Halloween dance with wrist bands attached. A congratulations card, written by Jade.* Sander peeked into the card, reading its inscription:

You are going to kill it at Nationals. I can't debate that! Love, Jade

Sander got a glimpse into their entire lives, which was

plastered all over the room. Posters of '80s movies, actors from the latest teen drama, a multitude of photos, trinkets, and memorabilia all traced the room, spilling over to Jade's side. One photo caught his eye as he appreciated that time had been frozen on the wall. An enlarged photo of Jade stared at him. She wore a Boston University sweatshirt as she held her acceptance letter, with a gigantic smile painted on her face. Pearl was peeking behind her in the photo, smiling with two thumbs up. Sander found himself drawn to the photo—the happiness, the support, the sisterhood. Their relationship hit him square in the face. His heart hurt for Pearl.

Pearl moaned as she woke from her nap, snapping him out of his moment. She smiled when he sat beside her on her bed.

"Welcome to my room."

"It's glorious. A person's bedroom says a lot about them. Yours tells a grand story."

Pearl blushed. "Thanks. Memories keep us going, right?"

"They sure do."

Sander refrained from asking about certain pieces he admired.

Pearl agreed to place the top hat in a small trinket box on her nightstand. As Sander stood to depart from the room, Pearl reached out her hand and said, "Please stay until I fall asleep.

Please?" He complied and approached the bedside. She patted her bed behind her, and he reluctantly followed her command. He positioned himself behind Pearl and wrapped his right arm around her waist. Her breathing slowed until she fell asleep.

A warming sensation built up in Sander's chest as he laid there with her, taking in her sorrow and imagining her life before all of this had happened to her. He did not immediately leave.

"I wish I could take all your pain away," he whispered.

Instinctively, Sander found himself inhaling the scent of Moroccan oil, which infused his senses as he squeezed her tighter. Pearl breathed out deeply, and he realized he was clutching her too hard. Sander glanced up at the alarm clock to see that it was 11:11 P.M. He leaned into her ear and whispered, "Its 11:11, Pearl, make a wish," and then kissed her softly on the cheek. Pearl gave no response, so he gently released his grip and slid himself off the bed. As he departed from the room, he felt twisted inside over falling for her.

"I promise to enjoy all the time we have together until there is no time left. Sleep well, dearest Pearl." He shut the door, concealing the darkness that Pearl had become accustomed to in the past months, and made his way down to the living room.

"How is she doing?" Marlene asked as Sander entered the living room.

"She's sleeping now, but it's all taken a toll on her,"

Sander said.

Jeff stepped forward and embraced Sander, "Thank you for everything you have done for her, Sander. We are very grateful to have you in our lives."

"I do what I can. I know what it is like to lose someone at a young age. Some days are good, and you think you can do it, then, suddenly, things crash down, and you don't know if you will make it through the next hour."

"If she would only allow us to help her, then maybe she could get better," Marlene said.

"Depression and grief can be tricky," Sander said. "When it has its grips on you, it can take hold and never let you go."

"Death. Such a terrible thing to discuss," Jeff said.

"Yes, I know. But letting her know you are there will make all the difference," Sander said.

"It amazes me how you know so much," Marlene said. "You must have a very old soul."

"I've been told," Sander said. "Mr. and Mrs. Juarez, I must be on my way. It's been an eventful evening, and I need to get some sleep. You two get some rest as well, okay?"

Jeff and Marlene nodded in agreement and escorted Sander to the front door. He stood on the front porch glancing at Pearl's window. Concern filled his heart. "Sweet dreams, Pearl. Catch ya later." Sander blew a kiss to Pearl's window as he did an about-face and headed into the abyss of the night.

THIRTEEN

Jade skipped into Group with a beaming smile.

"Aren't you a bundle of sunshine today," Chase commented.

"Yep, I get to go on my second visit in two days, and I couldn't be more excited."

"Wow, that's awesome," Emerick chimed in.

Jade glanced over at Emerick and shot him two thumbs up with a half-open smile.

Group had continued in its pattern of stories and support, with members arriving and departing, a new dynamic each session. Jade listened intently to what members shared and bounced in on occasion to provide supportive words.

"It's great you recognize it wasn't your fault, Yousef."

"I remember middle school too, Melissa. It was the

worst. So frustrating."

Chase beamed at her level of participation.

Jade took her turn, sharing about her upcoming visit.

"What are you looking forward to the most about this visit, Jade?" Chase asked.

"I've learned a lot through this group, Chase, but it didn't hit me until Ezekiel left…" Jade paused, recognizing for the first time that he wasn't sitting with her in Group. "Sorry... I lost my train of thought for a second. He taught me that I can't be truly happy until I work through it and progress as I need to. He helped me realize that I need to discover the cause of my death to move on, not just sit here and pout about the fact that, for some reason, I can't remember. Knowing tidbits so far has helped."

"I'll ask again, Jade. What are you looking forward to the most about your visit?" Chase asked.

Isn't it obvious? "Seeing Pearl. I'm hoping for more insight into what happened. I'm focused right now to understand and process what happened, and I can't wait to see her. I'll go while she is in Group this Saturday," Jade said.

"I think this is a good choice. Do you think she will reveal what you need to know?"

"I think she will. I truly do. I'm sure she misses me and is making progress in her own therapy, right?"

Chase became silent. "The thing about visits, Jade, is we need to make sure there is a level of open-mindedness to what we may come across. Your first visit was a short one, right?"

Jade nodded.

"If not used wisely, this one will also go by quickly. Your goal is to find out what happened to you. Listen to everything Pearl says. It will come out. Trust me."

"Right. Listen hard. Get the details. You got it, Chase. I'm excited about this step in my progress. I didn't think I would ever get here."

"You seem surprised," Chase commented.

"Getting stuck in your brain sucks. It's hard to explain. Kind of like when you experience a break-up and your brain struggles to see the brighter side of things."

"Yes…go on," Chase said.

"To me, it's what this process has been like—a break-up. I didn't want to deal with it and hoped the pain would go away on its own. But it didn't. If anything, it got worse, the harder I tried to push it away. I realize now that I can't push the pain away, or it will grow inside me like a virus. To get better, I need to work through this break-up, which is what I am trying to do now. Finally. Took me long enough."

"Profound insight," Jessica commented.

"Hey, all we have here is time," Chase commented.

"Good point, Chase. But I'd like to spend the rest of mine with Ezekiel, so I best get on with it," Jade said.

The group chuckled.

Jade laughed. "But in all seriousness, I'm doing this for me."

"Well done," Emerick said.

"Great," James added.

"Group, as you know, we make announcements when we have members complete their progress and are ready to move on. On their request, of course. This session, I am proud to announce that Emerick will be moving on as he has finished his progress."

"Wow, Emerick. I am so happy for you," Jade said.

Emerick smiled, "It's good to be content."

……

Jade soaked in the afternoon breeze in the garden following Group. Laying on the bench that she and Ezekiel had shared numerous times, she thought about how today seemed extra peaceful to reminisce. Laying there in the garden for the first time since Ezekiel left, she recalled their time together. The memories calmed her, igniting laughter and smile.

"Mind if I sit down?" A voice announced from behind the bench.

Jade opened her eyes and pivoted her head to see an upside-down image of Emerick. "Oh. Hey, Em. Sure, no problem. How's it going? When are you heading out of here?"

"Soon. I heard this place carried a peaceful quality about it, but dang it makes me want to do some serious meditating," Emerick said.

"I'm amazed by how fast you made progress. What is the key?"

"I think it helped knowing that my fate was on the horizon. I prepared myself just in case I didn't wake up the next morning—for years, that was my plan. My parents and I did a lot of prep work once I made it to ten, and every year after that became an extra blessing. When my health declined, we started getting closure. It's interesting when you can say your goodbyes before you say goodbye. Know what I mean, jelly bean?"

Not really. "Sure."

"There we were—me expressing gratitude to my parents, telling them how pleasurable it had been to be their son; them telling me how thankful they were to be my parents. There were no issues, no regrets. Everything pulled together in the end. I believe this is what helped us all get closure. Now I can move on at peace. I think your closure will come once you see your sister and finally understand how you died. You don't talk about your parents or other siblings much, so there must not have been an issue with them," Emerick said.

He's right, but why would he think that?

"I envy your experience saying goodbye. The suddenness of my death has me wondering how my family coped. You're right on one point. I did not have issues with my parents. But I feel gutted that I couldn't give them a hug or departing words before leaving. A consequence of my actions, I suppose. There's the irony."

"Sorry. I didn't mean to hit a nerve. Someone asked me once if I thought a sudden death would be worse than a slow, gradual one. Honestly, both would be just as bad for me. One doesn't allow for a goodbye, while the other forces you to fit things in that will never fit. It's a lose-lose situation."

Tell me about it. "Don't worry. You didn't hit a nerve. As far as Pearl, from what I gather, she and I were together the night I died. We always hung out like two peas in a pod, so it makes sense she was there. She did say over and over the night of my first visit, 'It's not your fault, Pearl,' so maybe something happened to me in front of her."

Her pupils fixed as she was hit with a flashback of Pearl laughing, wearing her favorite emerald green pea coat, trying to do their secret handshake with her and unsuccessfully completing it in a drunken stupor. She could hear herself laughing but couldn't see much of her surroundings. She did know they were outside in someone's backyard, steam exiting her mouth as she breathed. She could also see red plastic cups, which formed a triangle on the table as Pearl continually dropped her ping pong ball during the handshake debauchery.

“Crap, Emerick, she was there. I remember now… two pieces—me drunk, and her there with me. We were both drunk. That’s odd, Pearl rarely drinks.”

“Great, Jade. Keep going. Anything else pop in your head?”

Jade searched her brain, trying to pull anything else out that could be an indicator of her death, but she came up blank and shook her head, indicating this.

“Bummer. Saturday will be here soon enough,” Emerick said. “I’ll keep my fingers crossed for you. You’ll get there, I can feel it. Well, it’s my time now. Maybe I’ll see you soon?”

“If we have our way. Definitely.”

Emerick got up from the bench, shot Jade a smile, and began strolling down the rose path, soaking in the sun and observing everything around him. Jade knew his next stop. The ivy wall. That wall had a whole new meaning to her now, but she opted not to think about it.

I’ll get there one day. See you on the other side, Em.

Emerick had an exuberance about him that Jade didn’t quite understand. To see someone happy because they died struck her as a little off. *Then again, as he said, the fact that he made it this far is a good sign. Technically, he made it to old age in teen years*. He had helped her a great deal in going down the path towards knowing her fate, which made her feel grateful.

Saturday is only a few days away, and I can hardly stand it.

FOURTEEN

Following the Game Night incident, Pearl fell into the routine of sleeping in her room for an excessive amount of time. Secluding herself from the world became an art form for her over the past months, and people stopped attempting to bother her—except Sander, who made every attempt to reach out to Pearl in this state. Pearl opened her eyes to examine the phone, which had been beeping nonstop. The green and white text bubble flashed the number fifty-five; fifty-two of them from Sander, three from her mother. Pearl mustered up the energy to tap on the icon and release the texts shouting at her.

SANDR: How are you today?

SANDER: Hello?

SANDER: Pearl.

SANDER: Need to talk?

SANDER: Wake up.

SANDER: Lets hike.

SANDER: Miss you.

SANDER: XOXO.

Pearl didn't make it through the text parade before hearing a knock on her door. She knew it was Sander but didn't have the energy to tell him to go away. He didn't bother to knock a second time and invited himself into Pearl's room, a venti caramel macchiato in one hand, chai tea in the other.

Sander took a seat next to Pearl on the bed.

"Man, you stink," Sander said.

Go away. "Very funny, punk."

"Oh dang, she speaks. Ogre, let's get you out of the cave. What do you say? It's too lovely a Saturday to be wasting it indoors."

Pearl grimaced at the statement. *I hate it when he calls me ogre.*

"I'll take that as a 'yes.' Are you going to take your own shower, or do I need to have your mom come in and make sure you take one?"

Pearl sipped her tea then smacked him on the arm. "I can shower myself."

"Good, because the stench is starting to burn my nostrils."

Pearl giggled and rolled her eyes. *He's strong with the*

insults today. "Give me thirty minutes."

"Fine. Timer starts now."

Pearl didn't debate his gesture. She trusted that he would make sure she stays on task. She liked this about him. She *more* than liked it about him. Pearl arrived from the bathroom thirty minutes later. Sander had made her bed and cleaned her room.

"I asked your mom for some fabric freshener to spruce up this linen. Now you can smell like lavender fields when you sleep," Sander said.

"Oh joy," Pearl said. "Where are you planning to drag me today?"

"Let's start with the other side of this door," Sander said as he pointed at Pearl's bedroom door. "Then we can go from there."

Pearl shrugged her shoulders, then proceeded to follow Sander to the door. He stopped and extended his hand. "Are you ready?" Pearl reached out and clasped his hand, holding it tightly.

"Okay. Let's go," she said. In two steps, they were standing in the hallway.

"Good?"

"Yep."

"Want to try going down the stairs?"

"Sure."

Sander didn't let go of Pearl's hand as he guided her down the stairs and to the front door. He slowed down as they approached the front door, and Sander did another check-in with Pearl. "Outside of the house?" Pearl paused for a second then reluctantly nodded for Sander to continue his guided tour of the outside world. Sander reached into his pocket and pulled out a pair of sunglasses. "Here, you might need these until your eyes adjust to the light," he said with a smile.

"Oh, my word. Stop. I'm fine."

"Good. Let's go then."

They proceeded down the block. Sander talked about the weather and how unusually warm it was this time of year.

Who cares about the weather? "Sure. It's warm."

"Pearl. I need to talk to you about something."

"What's up?"

"I have cherished our time together. At first, I didn't want to share this with you, but I'm going to come out and say it. I like you."

Why didn't he want to share this with me? "I like you too."

"Cool."

"Like, *like* you, Sander."

Sander's eye widened. "What?"

"I *like*, like you, Sander."

"Why?"

"What?"

"Why?"

Pearl took a deep breath. "It's simple. You make me feel good. Normal. Like I'm not going through something. You don't put up with anything from me, and you are right there when something happens. It's almost like you were sent to be here with me," Pearl explained.

"Yes, I already told you that's why I'm here, sweetie." Sander winked at Pearl, hoping she wouldn't take his statement seriously.

She slapped him on the arm and giggled. "Oh, Sander."

They continued walking until they came to an intersection. Pearl noticed that the location looked similar. Engulfed in conversation, she failed to notice that Sander had taken her to group therapy. Pearl stayed quiet as she suddenly realized what Sander's plan for the day had been. He placed his hands on her shoulder and leaned into her left ear, whispering, "You can do this. I believe in you."

The warmth of his voice sent goosebumps, shooting down Pearl's arms and up her neck. She reached up and placed her left hand on her left shoulder, covering his hand. She gave his hand a small squeeze, tilting her head as her cheek met their joined hands. She lifted her head to confirm the reality that Sander had just presented to her. *Could I do this? What could it hurt? Come on, Pearl, suck it up and do it. You know you need this."* Pearl lowered her hand from Sander's grip, "Tell me again, Sander."

"You can do this." He leaned in and kissed Pearl on her cheek. She took one step forward onto the crosswalk with a new sense of focus on making it to Group with his support. Pearl took another step into the crosswalk, unaware that a car had just sped through the red light. Sander lunged forward and grabbed her by the arms, yanking her back to the sidewalk. They both fell to the concrete, Pearl landing on top of Sander. The two gazed into each other's eyes.

"What the heck, girl? You trying to get yourself killed?"

"No."

"I could never live with myself if you did."

"You saved my life." Pearl studied his face. His caramel eyes glistened as the sunlight struck them. Her fingertips pulsed restlessly on his chest as his grip tightened around her waist. Sander released his right hand from Pearl's waist and replaced it up around her neck, cradling her jawline. Pearl blinked her eyes repeatedly as she slowly lowered her lips to meet his. He supported her face as he lifted his head from the ground to kiss her back. Time stopped as they embraced each other, slowly kissing.

Where did you come from, Sander? Please don't ever leave

me. We found each other through the worst of circumstances, but we are the same; the same soul, same heart, body, mind, pain, happiness, sorrow, all wrapped up together in four arms, two people, and one kiss.

Pearl slowly pulled back from Sander, and the two opened their eyes to meet one another's gaze once more. Sander's eyes became saddened as he observed Pearl's misty eyes. He wiped a tear from her cheek with the back of his hand and commented, "I don't like seeing these."

"You bring me from the brink."

"I'd like you to stay away from the sadness, sweetie."

Easier said than done.

She pressed her palms on Sander's chest, pushing herself away from his body. "Group starts soon. We should get going." Pearl held out her hand to help Sander from the ground. As they waited for the crossing indicator to go on, Sander reached over and touched Pearl's hand. She smiled as the signal flashed.

This moment, forever.

As they arrived at the front door of Group, Sander placed his arm in front of Pearl, blocking her from entering the building. She glanced at him with a look of confusion on her face.

"Openness contributes to progress, Pearl. You can't have the second without doing the first. Remember that," he said.

I'm ready for this.

Pearl nodded and proceeded through the swinging door and down the hall to Group. She took her usual spot in the circle of chairs. Sander planted himself right next to her. The session began with a check-in on the previous week. A wave of sadness swallowed her as she prepared to speak. Her shoulders slumped as silence held her throat hostage. She didn't speak and reported nothing from the previous week.

Running into Henry at the football game, and the breakdown during Monopoly night. So much shame and despair. How can I share all of this? No improvement. Just a shell of a girl making zero progress. Another round closer to a total knockout in my life. Am I ever going to get better? Am I doomed to be this way even if I want to get better? It feels so hopeless.

Sander stared intently at her, igniting his words through her mind as her chest began knotting up. Pearl's hands gripped each other tightly. As her knuckles turned white and red, Sander reached over to alleviate the pressure. She glanced over at him feeling comforted as her anxiousness quickly flushed away. She took a deep breath and whispered, "I'm ready." She raised her hand and gained Albert's attention.

"Pearl. Would you like to share something?" Albert said.

You can do this. "Yes, I would," Pearl said. *Breathe.*

At first, Albert didn't know how to respond. After a few seconds, he regrouped and replied, "Whatever you're comfortable with sharing, we are here for you, Pearl."

Pearl took a deep breath.

You can do this. Just breathe.

"I've learned recently that openness contributes to progress."

Sander squeezed her hand.

"I know I haven't been a big participant here until now, but I realize that I don't want to be like this anymore. I am responsible for my own progress. So, I am ready to share my experience."

Silence and smiles filled the group. Eyes intently focused on Pearl, some waiting anxiously, others displaying sorrow.

Pearl's eyes focused on a coffee stain on the carpet below, threatening to touch her shoe. "We were together, my sister and I. Hanging with some friends. Drinking. We were drunk. Experimenting with some new 'stuff,' my friend, Henry, had brought. Innocent fun as usual. But that night, something happened."

"Stuff?" Albert asked.

Does this guy not know anything?

"Drugs. Henry supplied drugs to students at our school… underground. But being his friend at the time… I knew all about his business. He brought some new stuff and asked us if we wanted to try it. It looked unfamiliar to me, dark and powdery, like charcoal, packed in a capsule. He called it an 'upper.' Neither of us had done drugs before."

"You and Jade?"

"Yes. Me and Jade." *Just breathe.*

"I became hesitant to try it out—but not Jade. She had always pushed me to go farther with everything to 'get over my fears.' That night, I backed out because I began to grow paranoid. But Jade didn't and gave it a try. It didn't seem to affect her much at first, so we continued partying and having fun. But then, when we got home, things took a turn." Pearl ruffled her bun with her grip, tousling strands of hair in all directions.

"If I could only go back in time and change that night. I wouldn't be here now."

FIFTEEN

Jade awoke, eager to get dressed and out the door. The smile painted on her face was paired with the unstoppable tune she was whistling. *Felt like today would never come.* She raced down the hall to Adelaide's office and knocked vigorously on the door.

"All right, all right, I hear ya," Adelaide said as she made her way to the door and opened it.

"Are you ready, Adelaide? What time are we leaving? How long can I stay? Sorry, I'm excited."

"Darling, I have us scheduled to leave in the next few minutes. Group has started already. If we leave soon, we'll get there right after beginning intros and check-in."

Why can't we just get there now? "Fine, whatever, as long as we leave soon before I burst."

"Okay, let me get my things, and we will be all set." Adelaide opened the top right drawer to reveal the amulet. Placing it around her neck, Adelaide glanced at Jade and smiled. She approached Jade and held out the amulet for her to touch. "Okay, you remember how we did this last time, right?"

"Sure do," Jade said as she reached up and grasped the amulet. The room fell silent as the two stood concentrating on their impending destination. Jade took a deep breath and closed her eyes, exhaling deeply. When she opened her eyes, she and Adelaide were standing in a hallway with no lights for passage. Jade noticed a glare projecting from under a door thirty feet ahead. She continued down the hallway and peeked inside the room. A group of people were sitting, arranged in a circle.

Jade didn't immediately see Pearl, but she did notice a girl sitting with her back to the door, her hair in a messy bun, speaking while the rest of the group listened intently. Jade focused her ears on the conversation and immediately recognized a voice she had known her entire life. Pearl. Jade could vaguely hear what she was saying.

"That night, I backed out because I began to grow paranoid. But Jade didn't and gave it a try. It didn't seem to affect her much at first, so we continued partying and having fun. But then, when we got home, things took a turn."

Jade glanced at Adelaide, who motioned for her to

proceed into the room. She gulped hard, forcing the knot in her throat deep down into her stomach, and took a step forward, followed by another, until she stood five feet from Pearl.

"Everything seemed normal. I drove us home. Jade had a strong buzz, and I had a little buzz going. I can't believe I drove us home buzzed." Pearl grunted, choking on her words like they were venom to her soul. *Everyone must think I am so irresponsible.*

"We got home and stumbled up the stairs to our room. Mom and Dad had gone on a couple's retreat for the weekend, so sneaking in and getting caught wasn't a worry. So, there we were in the room, giggling about who knows what—when we get into our modes, everything's funny. I thought she was okay. At some point, she passed out in her bed, and I, in mine. But then I heard gurgling. I got up to turn Jade on her side, thinking she was getting sick, but that wasn't the case," Pearl continued, her eyes glossing over.

Jade proceeded through the group until she was standing in front of Pearl. Gazing at her, she was shocked at what she saw. A skeletal face, the result of an apparent double-digit pound loss over the past few months. The dark half-moons under Pearl's eyes glared through her makeup and spoke volumes as to how much Pearl must have slept, or *not* slept, in quite some time. Pearl's lips were chapped, and her skin translucent. She repeatedly pulled her sweater up to her shoulder; it was unable to hang onto her now extremely petite frame.

What happened to her? This can't be real. Jade wanted to hug Pearl but knew her only option was listening.

Pearl became quiet. Jade scanned the group members and spotted a face she had seen before. The gentleman sitting next to Pearl held her hand as she cried. He sat tall with porcelain skin, black hair, and caramel eyes with little speckles of black. Jade's memory flashed to this stranger opening the door of Adelaide's office.

Sander.

He fixed his attention over to Jade. Nodding his head to her, he resumed his duty of consoling Pearl as she sat there crying about what she had just shared. "You can stop if you want," Sander notified Pearl.

"No, I have to do this," Pearl said. She fanned her hands on her face, breathed in deeply, and continued. "I turned the light on to see my sister lying there convulsing, foam spewing from her mouth. I panicked and ran to turn her onto her side, but it didn't help. I yelled for Mom and Dad but forgot they weren't there. They weren't going to be back for another day." Pearl began rubbing her fingers through her hair, loosening the bun on her head. "Her eyes were fixed in an upward position like she was trying to look at her own eyelids but couldn't manage. It felt like forever. Then, suddenly, it stopped. After wiping everything off her, I noticed that her breathing had stopped, so I tried doing CPR. I could hear her in my head saying, 'Faster, Pearl, faster. Keep going, don't stop. Save me. Please save me.'"

Jade's eyes flashed, pressure jolted in her temple. She crouched down and shook her head to release the pain. Instead, a visual formed. "I see it. Everything she is saying I'm seeing right now. It's like a movie. Now, I remember. I remember, Adelaide." Fear was painted all over Jade's face.

Adelaide pressed back, "Keep going."

Pearl continued, "I called 9-1-1 and continued doing CPR. I didn't know what else to do."

Pearl bear-hugged herself as she closed her eyes. "I gripped her so tight I could feel my own circulation getting cut off. I thought that if I squeezed her harder, maybe she wouldn't slip away; maybe my arms would keep her alive until help came. But she felt heavier and heavier by the second. I quickly became unable to hold her anymore because she weighed as heavy as a bag of cement." Pearl paused.

The room fell silent as participants listened in disbelief and horror. A single sniffle could be heard in the distance. Pearl released herself from her own embrace as her eyes wandered up to the lights.

"She died on the way to the hospital, but I found out later

that she was already brain dead while I was doing CPR. I had to call Mom and Dad to tell them what happened. Can you imagine having to come home from vacation because your senseless daughters were stupid, and one of them died?"

Jade couldn't believe what she had just heard. She stood in disbelief, shocked that she had forgotten this information. Pearl began trembling—first her knees then her hands—as she stayed quiet, trying to control her breathing.

Sander rubbed her back in a circular motion saying, "It's okay, sweetie. You're doing great."

"I felt responsible. It was my friend who gave her the drugs. At her funeral, someone told me that before we left the party, he gave her a few ecstasy pills. I know she took one before we left. I guess the overdose kicked in when she took a second pill after we got home." Pearl rubbed her scalp until her bun lost its shape and cascaded down her back. Her face, heavy with misery, fell into her palms, which masked it in shame. Her skin was pulsing red as rage built up in her chest until she couldn't hold it in anymore. "How could I be so stupid!"

Members jolted in their seats at her blast of words. Looks of confusion and fear covered their faces as they attempted to process what had just unfolded before them. Albert froze as Jade ran to Pearl and fell to her knees.

"I don't blame you, Pearl," she choked, tears streaming

down her face. "I'm sorry. I'm so sorry."

Adelaide watched from the door but made no move to deter Jade's behavior.

"If you could tell your sister anything, Pearl, what would you say?" Albert asked.

"I'm sorry." She whimpered through her fingers.

Jade and Sander exchanged looks as he shook his head. He continued rubbing Pearl's back. Pearl paid no attention to the gesture and continued whispering, "I'm sorry. I'm sorry."

"Mind if I escort her out for a few minutes?" Sander asked Albert.

"Please."

Sander lifted Pearl by the arm to guide her to the door, but she couldn't move or stop crying. Her breathing became erratic as she started to sweat. Sander requested that the hospital be called to assist. Albert pulled out his phone, and with one touch of the screen, he contacted the paramedics. Sander approached Adelaide and whispered in her direction. Jade couldn't see his face, but Adelaide's raised eyebrows and frown gave an indication of what he had said.

Jade focused her attention back at her sobbing sister and wished she had the power to allow Pearl to hear and feel her.

It's frustrating knowing my death caused so much pain. She could no longer bear seeing her sister this way.

I can't believe I did this to her.

Jade stood up and faced Adelaide. "I want to go home."

"We've only been here a few minutes. If we don't stay the entire time, you jeopardize your final visit. See this out, Jade."

"I want to go back. Now. What good am I here? Yes, I found out what happened to me, but at what cost? Look at her… look at her!" Jade shouted, pointing at the frail girl sobbing next to her. "I can't even feel her. I want nothing but to take her pain away, but I can't. This whole experience has been absolute torture for me. Did you know about this?"

Adelaide didn't respond. Jade turned her fury to Sander. *He did.* "You did. What have you done to help? From where I'm standing, you haven't done much, have you?" Jade approached Sander and continued her tirade. "Some Guardian Energy you are. If you did your job, she wouldn't be in this state. What did you do to help?"

"I…" Sander mustered.

"Answer me!" Jade shouted as she shoved Sander in the chest. Her breath escaped her as she stood there, her eyes wide in shock that she had just shoved him to the ground. The group glanced over as Sander recovered himself from the floor and adjusted his shirt.

"Are you okay, Sander?" Albert asked.

"Yes, I'm fine. I just stumbled over my feet." He shot a

dagger stare to Jade, who was still in shock by her actions.

"We are leaving now," Adelaide said. *Good.* Jade held out her hand and took hold of the amulet, glancing back at Pearl before closing her eyes. *I can't believe I did this to you. Please forgive me.*

When she opened her eyes, they were back in Adelaide's office.

……

Jade felt heavy as she slumped in Adelaide's office chair.

"What were you thinking? Do you realize what you've done?" Adelaide questioned.

He deserved it.

Jade sat motionless and speechless. Adelaide, standing by her desk, leaned against the front of her desk with her arms crossed and eyebrows furrowed directly at Jade. It reminded Jade of the time she had gotten into trouble for ditching school on Senior Ditch Day, her freshman year. "When were you going to tell me about Sander?" Jade asked.

"Right now, this isn't about him. Right now, we need to discuss what will happen to you because of this catastrophe you caused."

"What do you mean?"

"You physically assaulted a staff member. That's grounds for immediate termination of any further visits. You leave me no choice here, Jade, but to cancel your final visit."

"What?" Jade protested. "That's not fair. How could you do this to me? This is all I have left to help me progress."

"My hands are tied. It must be documented and handled accordingly. I really am sorry, Jade."

Jade catapulted from her seat, "This is bullshit. You take me to this Group session, knowing that Sander will be there, and don't say anything to me about it. Why didn't you tell me about him?"

"You didn't need to know about him. He's not part of your program. He's doing the best he can to help Pearl out. It's been a struggle."

Help? What a crock.

"Tell me the details. What exactly is he doing for her?"

"I can't discuss that with you."

"Oh, come on, you're kidding me. It's my sister. How could it be off-limits for me to know what happens to her?"

"Because it is. And that's that. I know you're upset, but you and Pearl are two separate issues. I can't share with you what is going on with her, and Sander can't blow his cover. It's a delicate situation we are dealing with, and I need you to understand that we have her best interests in mind… along with yours."

"But why wouldn't you say anything to me? At least

about my sister. It makes no sense."

"Not everything in life makes sense."

"*You* don't make sense."

"Meaning?"

"What are you actually here for? To help me? To look out for me? It doesn't seem like it. All you've done is push me to keep going to Group, but what are you doing *for* me? You won't even tell me what happens if I don't make progress. You always stall when I bring up that subject."

Adelaide remained silent.

"Why don't you answer me? What happens if I don't progress. You know something, don't you?"

"I… need you to keep progressing. It's important. You don't want to…"

"What? Go somewhere else?"

"It's not so simple."

"Do I disappear into oblivion?"

"Jade."

"Seems pretty simple. I have to go somewhere, right?"

Adelaide's jaw tightened as she clenched her teeth.

"What? Answer me, please. Give me some insight, please. I'm over not knowing anymore."

Adelaide could no longer hold her thoughts. "You don't go anywhere."

Jade's pupils dilated. *What did she just say?* "You don't go anywhere? What does that even mean?"

"If you don't progress, you don't go anywhere. You stay right here. You've got your answer. I know this because it happened to me.

Jade's eyes widened, "are you serious? Oh, Adelaide."

"I like helping people, but staying here did not initially solicit my interest. I was so angered by my death, that even thinking about coming to terms with it never interested me. And before I knew it, I was not able to leave. I'll never know what it's like to move on, and that's my fault. But it won't be yours because you will finish the program and move on. You just have to."

"I'm sorry. I didn't know. I…"

"Nobody does. As far as I know, I'm the only one here that has experienced this. I really do love what I do. Helping you all gives me a great sense of fulfillment. And I don't want to see you harbor feelings the way I did."

"I think I've worked well on getting those out."

"That, I definitely agree with. You've changed, Jade Juarez. For the better. Now, about your sister. Do you have anything else you would like to share about today?"

"I'm mixed on how I feel about what happened," Jade said

"Fair enough," Adelaide said. "Want to share why?"

"I hated seeing her so fragile, weak, tired, and broken down. To know that she's in this condition because of me makes my heart hurt. I hate knowing I did this to her. That *I* caused her this pain and agony."

"Sander is supporting. Hopefully, he can help turn her around."

"I still can't do my third visit?"

"Oh, honey. Unfortunately, no."

"He will save her, won't he?"

"It's hard to say. He will do his best."

Jade collapsed into the chair. *How can this be? On the one hand, it comforted me watching Sander there with Pearl—he's so patient and kind. In a way, I guess he is helping. She has someone. Jade, don't look at it too hard.*

"You didn't cause it, Jade. You need to know this."

"Oh, I didn't, did I? My sister is depressed because her sister died. Her sister being me. How can I not feel responsible? As helpful as it is learning facts about how I died, the agony of knowing what happened makes my stomach turn. Knowing gets me one step closer, I know, but coming to terms with my death is what I am struggling with right now. How can I come to terms with knowing I left carnage behind?" Jade stopped talking and averted her eyes from Adelaide as she cried into her sleeve.

"Why were they so important?" Adelaide asked.

"Why were what so important?"

"The drugs. What was the importance of them when you took them?"

Don't lie. It'll get you nowhere now.

"Something new. I was an athlete and had always been clean. I was going places and didn't want anything to jeopardize my goals. I was told never to test dirty if they test me, so I had to stay clean. But as school neared the end of the year, I guess I saw that as my free pass to have the experience just once. I really wish I could take it back. I ruined everything. My future, Pearl, my family. All of it. It's all my fault."

Adelaide approached Jade and knelt next to her, placing her hand on Jade's knee.

"Hey, look at me," she said.

No.

"Look at me."

Jade obeyed her request and looked up.

"This isn't your fault. Don't blame yourself. There is one tool you can use to see how Pearl is doing." Adelaide proceeded to pull the amulet from her pocket and then placed it in Jade's hand. "Although you don't have any more visits left, when you hold this and think about the person you want to see, they will appear. But be careful—if it breaks, it will not work, and it cannot be fixed or replaced."

Jade shook her head and squeezed the amulet while thinking of Pearl. She stared intently into the amulet as a vision of Pearl began appearing through the clouded glass. Propped up in a hospital bed, she gazed out of the window in a daze. Next to her were four bottles of medication. Jade's parents were there—her mother was holding Pearl's hand and crying, while her father was rubbing her mother's shoulders, telling her it will be okay. *She's safe for now. I hope it stays that way.*

"Something wrong?" Adelaide asked, noticing the change in Jade's breathing.

"It's… it's nice to see her calm. She looks angelic," Jade said.

As Jade finished speaking, Adelaide received a text and grabbed her phone from her pocket.

SANDER: 5150. WILL DISCUSS WITH YOU LATER.

Adelaide quickly placed her phone back in her pocket.

"What's that?"

"Oh, my reminder text about an appointment tomorrow."

"Oh."

"Jade, how do you feel about this visit, and how do you think it has helped with your recovery?"

"Mixed. I'm glad I got what I needed, but honestly, seeing her like that was a little…"

"Little…?"

"Disturbing."

"I see how it could make you feel that way. Pearl is stable now, and you can look in on her whenever you want, so maybe that will help."

"Can I take it with me when I move on?"

"Unfortunately, no."

"Bummer. It's been an exhausting experience. I think I'm going to take a walk through the garden."

"Sounds like a good idea, dear. Enjoy."

Jade disappeared down the hall and into the garden. She couldn't help but think about what she needed right now… Ezekiel. A hug and reassurance from him would have been perfect right now. It would have helped her process what happened today—his arms wrapped around her, squeezing all the fear and doubt from her soul, melting everything away.

Someday.

Process. How to process this. Let's see. Jade pulled out her journal from her satchel and made a list:

1) Drinking (drunk)
2) I took drugs (took drugs)
3) I had what looked like a seizure or overdose (seizure or overdose)

4) Pearl's guilt lies in knowing that Henry gave them to me (Pearl's guilt). He's her friend, so I can understand that. She needs to work it out, and I'm sure she will someday. I need to worry about me. I feel guilty saying this, but deep down, I know I won't recover by focusing on others.

You can do this, Jade.

She grabbed the amulet and closed her eyes, preparing to see what the whimsical cloud would show her next.

SIXTEEN

Pearl fluttered her eyes open to the afternoon sun. She had been at the hospital for three days, and her legs were restless from her recumbent state. Sander sat by her side as she awoke, like he had done every day since her admission.

"Good morning," Sander greeted.

She shifted her attention to him in a groggy fashion. She adjusted herself upright, yawned, and smiled in response to Sander's greeting. "Morning, Sander."

"How are we feeling today?"

"Less depressed than a few days ago."

"That's good to hear."

"We can count that as a plus," Sander said, reaching forward and moving strands of hair from Pearl's face to reveal her sunken features.

Pearl giggled. “I am good to go home today, aren’t I?”

“If the doctor deems you good to go, then yes, we can take you home,” Sander said.

He makes me feel safe. Like I belong to him. He really does like protecting me.

“Thank you, Sander.”

“For what?”

“Being you.”

Sander leaned in and took Pearl into his arms. “Thanks for *letting* me be me.”

Dr. Watson arrived and evaluated Pearl, clearing her to be discharged. Leaving the hospital with a new sense of freedom, Sander and Pearl parted ways with Marlene and Jeff and headed to Scoop a Dee’s for some ice cream.

Pearl appeared happy, but Sander knew that this would not last, knowing he would have to leave soon. He had met with Adelaide before arriving at the hospital, and they agreed that the best solution would be to remove him from the situation and bring in another guardian. Although Sander protested at first, in the end, he knew that he had become too involved, which violated protocol.

He stared down at his bowl, tracing designs into the melting ice cream with his spoon. But he never took a bite.

“Hey. Why the long face?” Pearl asked. “I’m the

depressed one here, not you."

"I… I… I… need to share something with you," Sander said as he released his grip from the spoon and replaced it with Pearl's hand.

"What is it?" Pearl asked.

Sander paused. Heat built up in his cheeks. He stared into Pearl's eyes and could only feel guilty for having to leave. He knew it would ruin the moment, but he also knew it needed to be done. *But does it have to be right now?* Thinking quickly, Sander bought himself some extra time by avoiding the subject.

"I care about you a lot, Pearl. I wanted you to know that. You *do* know. Right, Pearl?"

"Yes, of course, I do."

"Good. Let's finish this ice cream before it all melts." Sander glanced down at his bowl of ice cream soup.

"Oops, too late," Pearl said.

"Bad timing," Sander said as he carried the bowl to the garbage can and tossed it in.

Bad timing indeed.

SEVENTEEN

Jade enjoyed watching her family in the amulet—Andrew skateboarding; Pearl enjoying ice cream with Sander; her mom and dad cooking Sunday breakfast and laughing like they used to do. She felt a level of content, knowing they were doing okay.

I wonder when the process will happen for me to move on? I'm making progress every session, and I'm feeling much better.

Chase pulled her aside one day after Group to tell her how elated it made him that she continued doing so great in

Group. “Thanks. I guess it’s just a waiting game now. Hopefully, I will leave soon,” she replied.

She continued with her journal entries.

Today I am feeling great. Pearl looks to be doing better, so does Mom, Dad, and Andrew. Jamie is killing it in football. Everything seems great all around. What will happen next? I wonder if I am missing something since I haven't moved on yet. Patience is a virtue, right?

Jade’s entry made her think about the effect she had on people.

Are people happy because I became easy to forget? Or are they happy because they know I would have wanted them to be happy?

Jade stared into the amulet.

I wonder what Zeek is doing right now. Is he thinking of me? Of us? Would he appear here if I concentrate on him?

She closed her eyes and concentrated. The amulet billowed as Jade opened her eyes and stared intently into it, watching the smoke move vigorously in a circular motion over and over and over… but no Ezekiel. She waited some more to see if he would appear, but nothing.

Damn.

“Soon,” Jade whispered to herself. “Soon.”

EIGHTEEN

Pearl and Sander sat on the lake, admiring the ripples created in the water by the pebbles they tossed. Occasionally, they attempted to skip the pebbles across the water but concluded they weren't good at this part.

"Sander, you ever wish you could be something other than what you are now?"

"Meaning?"

"I look around and wonder why it is so difficult to be human. I wonder if animals and fish experience depression. Like, when a fish gets killed, do the other fish in their school get depressed? It doesn't seem like it. The fish seem to move on because it's what they must do for survival. So, why is it so difficult for our species to do this?"

"Miss Philosophical. I'm not sure I'm qualified to answer. That's above my pay grade. But if I had to guess, I would say maybe it's because the human brain is more complex. Animals and fish have much simpler brains, and all they are capable of doing is making sure they stay alive. While humans are able to think about much more… and therefore *feel* much more. And that allows us to feel deeply for one another and get attached. I imagine that these things present pretty substantial barriers to recovery."

Animals and fish have feelings too.

Pearl grabbed another pebble and tossed it into the water.

"Look." Sander pointed at the water. "Look at the ripples."

Pearl followed Sander's request and stared at the rippling water. "The pebble is your emotions; the water is you. You allow them to cause a ripple in your life. But with tools and support, what happens? Eventually, the ripples disappear, and you're left with calm water."

"You mean, calm emotions."

Sander chuckled. "Yes, sweetie."

Why is that funny? "I feel like I don't belong here. Like this place isn't for me. It's hard to explain because I don't know where I belong, but it doesn't feel like I belong here." Pearl shared.

"Have you always felt this, Pearl?"

"Not until recently. I don't want to say everything changed because of Jade, but with her not here, I feel so incomplete. I feel lost and broken."

Pearl threw another pebble in the water. It did not skip. She wiped a tear from her cheek with her middle finger.

"You'll find your somewhere soon. Maybe that's what you need."

He's not understanding me.

"Yeah. Maybe."

Sander's chest tightened. He immediately drew back from the conversation.

He's acting odd all of a sudden. "What's wrong?"

"I… there… um…" Sander stumbled. He turned his back to Pearl, hoping she wouldn't see the beads of sweat formulating on his brow.

"Please just tell me what you need to say. I can handle

it."

"I'm not sure, darling."

Pearl reached over and grabbed him by the bicep, yanking him towards her until he faced her, half-tilted, leaning on her shoulder. "Sander, if you don't tell me what you want to say right this moment, I swear, you will be the unhappiest man in the whole..."

"I am leaving," Sander blurted out. His fear and nervousness inadvertently caused word vomit.

What? Pearl released her grip from him and sat there in silence. Sander didn't bother asking her to respond.

Pearl slowly raised herself from her sitting position and walked into the woods. Sander followed her, just paces behind as she tripped along in a zombie-like fashion, weaving through the forest of trees. She suddenly halted her stride as if an invisible wall prevented her from passing through, and dropped to her knees, surrendering her face into her palms.

Sander ran to meet up with her and dropped to his knees as well, wrapping his arms around her.

"How could you be leaving?" Pearl whimpered. "Where are you going?"

Sander knew he needed to fib. "Hey, hey, hey. I'm only leaving Group. I have work obligation and can't go anymore."

Why didn't he say this in the first place? Pearl exhaled

heavily, a small grin formulating on her face.

"Before I met you, I wandered through this life, thinking that happiness would never come my way. Sure, I helped people, which gave me fulfillment; but the connection I have with you, Pearl, I don't think I will ever have again."

Stop confusing me.

"You're talking like you're leaving forever, Sander. I can still contact you by phone, right? We are still going to hang out, right? Right?"

"Don't be silly with that talk. Of course, we will hang out."

Relieved, Pearl released the tension in her body and tapped his forearm.

The two embraced each other once more before retreating to their initial location near the water.

Pearl leaned her head on Sander's shoulder and said nothing. They watched as the horizon engulfed the sun, leaving behind rays of gold and pink in the pale blue sky.

"You're kind of like my sun, Sander."

"How so?"

You can't figure it out? "You bring warmth and brightness into my life and, even during moments when you aren't around, I still know you are there."

Sander leaned in and gave Pearl a kiss on the cheek.

"Come. I need to get you home," Sander said. He jumped to his feet and held out his hands to assist Pearl to her feet. The two strolled hand in hand back to their vehicle and climbed in.

The drive back to the house was quiet. The usual banter between the two was replaced with somber silence. Sander made his usual gesture—he reached over and held Pearl's hand as he drove through her neighborhood. The two arrived at her home shortly after. Sander turned off the ignition but didn't take out the keys.

I guess he won't be coming in. I don't get it.

Pearl lunged out of her seat and into his arms, pulling back tears when hugging him but saying nothing.

"You have a pleasant evening, my lovely," Sander said, squeezing her so tightly that he could feel the air quickly escaping from her mouth. He then gave one last kiss before she departed.

He watched her as she slowly faded from his life, sealed by the sound of the front door shutting. He's had goodbyes before, but this beat all of them on the level of difficulty. His throat dried his voice as his heartbeat pulsed in his temple at the urge to knock on the door and tell her he was a guardian spirit sent to protect her.

"Hopefully, I won't see you soon, my love. But eventually, I will, and I can definitely wait for that day."

He grabbed the car key, and reluctantly turned it forward

to start the car. He shifted into drive and drove away.

……

It had been a few days since Pearl communicated with Sander. She pulled out her phone and prepared to send him a text:

PEARL: Hola.

SANDER:

PEARL: Thinking of you. Text me back please.

SANDER:

PEARL: It's 11:11. Make a wish.

SANDER: Message undeliverable.

Those words shot through her heart, hemorrhaging it—twenty letters, delivering such agony in a millisecond.

"He doesn't want to see you anymore", is what she read. She let herself get swallowed up by the bed as the weight of the moment sank in.

What did I do wrong? Am I too needy? Maybe I am the side girl. Maybe he just got tired of me. Who could blame him? Why would he want to love me anyway? I'm a complete mess.

She looked down to notice her index finger had been entangled in her hair. She stared at the strands holding her finger hostage.

Tangled just like me. You need to be set free.

She rose from her bed and made her way to her

immaculately organized desk. The desk had not seen attention for a while and sat like an organized tomb, dust mounting around the sorted paperwork. She opened the bottom right drawer, revealing a pair of scissors sitting neatly in the middle of the drawer. She picked up the scissors and, in a swift snip, watched as her hair departed from her scalp and hung lifelessly from her fingers. Flicking her fingers, she watched as her hair fell to the floor.

Pearl glided over to the bathroom, pausing at the counter to evaluate the mess staring back at her in the mirror. Her eyes wandered over to the empty sink next to her that had not been touched in several months—Jade's sink. A flashback trespassed her mind and made Pearl smile. She remembered how during elementary school, they would race at their sinks while getting ready for school; the sister who completed her hair and teeth the fastest would hold dibs for the day on sitting in the front seat on the way to school.

But those memories were over now. Pearl returned her vision to herself and stared intently into the mirror.

What is it about me? What do people see? They see this. A mess. A tangled, stupid mess. I'm no good for anyone anymore, and neither is this hair.

She grasped a handful of hair and sliced away with the scissors until the hair fell free to the floor. Evaluating the newly chopped section, she took another handful, looped it around her hand, and began vigorously squeezing the scissors, watching clump after clump of hair make its way to the floor. She continued grabbing and cutting, and cutting, and cutting until her onyx hair hung eleven inches shorter, sitting just slightly below her ears. A new Pearl looked back in the mirror.

I still don't like it.

As she cut the last strand for the night, she nicked herself on the wrist with the scissor's edge. She stared intently at the open wound.

That didn't hurt at all.

She placed the entire scissor's edge on her wrist and stopped.

One motion, that's all it takes. One and this will all be over.

But in that moment, nobody went through her head; not her mom, her dad, Andrew, Jade, Sander, or Henry—nobody. She let go of the scissors and watched as they descended to the tile floor and landed in the pile of hair sitting lifelessly in front of the counter.

She gave herself one expressionless look in the mirror before retreating to her room, leaving the aftermath of hair and scissors on the floor. She crawled back into her bed and pulled the covers up over her head. She felt safe in the dark. Nobody bothered her in the dark. So, the dark is where she stayed.

Emotionally exhausted, Pearl fell asleep.

NINETEEN

Adelaide arrived at Jade's room with good news. "Good morning, sunshine. I've got some good news for you."

Jade sprouted up from her bed and nearly shook Adelaide into delirium from her excitement. "I got approved?!"

Adelaide nodded her head with a big smile on her face.

I got approved.

"Oh my goodness, this is such great news. I'm so freaking excited I can't contain myself. When will this all happen?"

"Not right away. There are some logistics I need to get into place, but then you will be good to go. Let's say about three to four days."

"Hey, it's better than never, am I right?"

"Now, I know what your decision will be, but I have to ask you anyway. There is an option here to stay and be a mentor if you are interested."

Move on to be with Ezekiel, of course.

"Why is this being offered to me?"

"We ask everyone. Some stay, some proceed."

"Tempting, but I prefer to move on."

"Figured as much. You can relax these next few days and let me handle all of the paperwork, okay? You only need to sign a few things, but that's it."

"Whatever works and gets me moving on, I'm all for it."

As Adelaide departed from the room, Jade reached over and grabbed her journal:

> *I'm moving on. I feel so ready. I can't express how happy I am right now. To see Zeek and give him the biggest hug of his life will be so awesome. Now, I get to tell him I love him! I can't contain myself right now. I'm so curious about what awaits me. I'm also a little nervous that I'll get there and not find anybody. I wonder if I will see Aunt Ellie. That would*

be cool.

……

Jade shared the good news with Chase, who seemed almost as excited as her when he found out.

Nothing could dim my vibe. I feel on top of the world.

She needed to keep busy, so she watched her family through the amulet. Mom and Dad traveled to Washington to watch Jamie play football. They looked proud, cheering on her big brother as he smashed Husky Skulls. Jade enjoyed spying on Andrew playing video games at home and giggling at him when he became angry.

This is good closure.

She was hesitant about looking in on Pearl since she didn't want to experience a repeat of Pearl's Group session.

I last saw her in a good place, but I need to know—I have to know. How can I possibly move on without seeing her?

She concentrated, thought of Pearl, and waited for the smoke to reveal what she wanted to see.

Pearl strolled down the neighboring street.

Cute hair. Short, but cute.

The houses were not from their street.

I wonder where she is heading?

Pearl held a small shoebox covered in buttons, blue and pink glitter, and stickers ranging from unicorns to a strawberry wearing sunglasses. She did recognize the box. A trinket box Pearl kept in her closet. Pearl and Henry made it in elementary school when they officially became friends. Jade never knew its contents but assumed it included notes, pictures, and other memorabilia. Pearl headed up a concrete path, followed by ten stairs. Then a second path ending at the front porch of a blue and white Victorian home. Pearl climbed three more stairs up to the porch and rang the doorbell.

Henry's house.

Henry's mother answered the door, her eyes forgetting to blink. A gaping hole replaced her mouth as she stared at Pearl. Pearl said nothing as the eye contact became excruciating.

"Pearl," she mustered.

"Good morning, Alice. Is Henry here?"

"Yes. He's up in his room. Won't you please come in?"

"No, thank you. I will wait for him out here."

Set back by Pearl's words, Henry's mother pursed her lips and stared. She turned her head away and called out, "Henry! You have a visitor."

"Be right down!" Henry shouted from upstairs. It took a few minutes for him to appear at the front door. His greeting was silenced as he stared at Pearl, a look of confusion on his face.

Pearl cleared her throat, "Henry."

"Pearl, what are you doing here?"

"I came to bring you this," Pearl said, holding the box out for him to see. "I want to give it to you."

"To me? Why?"

"Because I want you to have it. I don't blame you anymore."

She knew Pearl cared a great deal about the friendship box and protected it. For her to give it up didn't sit right with Jade.

Maybe giving the box to Henry is helping her heal. It just seems off that she is giving it away. She always cherished that box.

"Would you like to come in?"

"No thanks, Henry. I must get going. I just wanted to make sure you have this."

She stepped back and swiveled around to begin her descent down the steps. She halted her stride when she heard, "Pearl." She turned around to see Henry bolting out the front door and heading straight toward her. He wrapped his arms around her, squeezing tightly. "You'll always be my friend. I adore you. I hope you remember this."

Pearl's arms remained at her side as she didn't attempt to squeeze him back. "I know. Take care."

Henry released his grip as the distance increased between the two of them. He stood there engaged in a thousand-yard stare, watching Pearl leave his lawn, their friendship, and his life.

Jade continued watching the amulet to pick up any emotional cues, but she couldn't. Pearl's stone-cold expression shot through Jade's chest as she proceeded down the street and through the neighborhood back home. Jade couldn't look away, completely immersed in thoughts about what her sister might do next. Once home, Pearl sat down at her desk and began writing. Jade couldn't see what she scribed, but she watched as Pearl spent a chunk of time doing it.

What on earth is she writing?

Pearl appeared calm and emotionless during her writing. She rose from the desk then headed to Andrew's room. She took a piece of paper and slid it under his door. She then proceeded down the hall to her parents' room, leaving another piece of paper on the dresser.

Okay, now I'm worried.

Jade exited her room, amulet in hand, intently watching Pearl's every move. She slowly made her way down the hall to Adelaide's office as she watched Pearl walk back to her bedroom and plop on her bed.

Pearl grabbed a medication bottle on her nightstand. She studied the bottle for a few minutes. "Take one daily for sleep." She took a deep breath, leaned over the side of her bed, and pulled out a bottle of Whiskey. "Dad won't miss this."

What the hell, Pearl.

Jade watched as Pearl emptied a pill into her hand, inserted it into her mouth, and then washed it down with a quick swig. Pearl then tilted the medication bottle once more, emptying six pills into her hand, and catapulted them into her mouth, chasing them with half the bottle of liquor.

I can't believe what I'm seeing. She's...

Jade clasped her hands to her mouth in shock, forgetting the amulet in her hand. She watched in slow motion as the amulet fell to the floor, shattering into pieces. Jade fell to her knees to examine the crystal demolition. "No!" she panicked, knowing she could no longer see Pearl or find out what will happen to her.

Jade exploded into an all-out sprint down the hallway, not bothering to knock on Adelaide's door as she stormed into her office. Adelaide and Sander were in the middle of a deep discussion.

"Jade," Adelaide said, her voice wobbly.

Sander stood up and grabbed Jade. "Jade. What is it? Is it Pearl? What?"

Jade attempted to say that Pearl had just ingested several sleeping pills, but the words never came.

"Is it Pearl?" Sander demanded. Jolting Jade with his grip. Jade nodded. He said nothing as he ran out the door.

"Don't worry. I assure you he's got her. He's not on the

case anymore, but he does have access to her." Adelaide assured Jade. "Please have a seat. Where is the amulet? I would like to see what has happened."

Jade managed to blurt out through the tears on her face, "Amulet broke, I dropped it while running here."

"Oh dear." Adelaide's eyes moved back and forth as she attempted to think of a solution. "I'm so sorry, Jade, but without the amulet, we cannot find out what has happened."

"Are you serious? There's no other way to see her?"

"I wish there were, darling, but the amulet had all the access you needed. The only thing we can do now is wait for Sander to get back. Hopefully, he will bring good news."

"What about another visit?"

"You lost your final one. I cannot change that. I really wish I could, but I can't. I'm so sorry, sweetie."

I can't believe I am hearing this right now.

Jade stood in a daze. Feeling blind, she wandered out of the office, not noticing Adelaide speaking to her until she heard, "Jade. Are you okay?" But Adelaide's words were muffled as though Jade's ears were stuffed with cotton balls.

"I have to go to my room now." Jade began her journey down the hall, still in a daze. Once inside her room, she collapsed onto her bed, curling into the fetal position. She hoped for the best result but knew she should prepare for the worst.

She'll be okay.

She'll be okay.

She's not okay.

She'll be okay.

TWENTY

The whiskey scorched Pearl's throat as she drowned herself in the taste. The pills passed like rocks down her esophagus, and she gagged twice in the process. She came up for air, inhaling fiercely as she dropped the bottle to the floor, the loud thump signaling her completion.

Pearl laid on her bed, gazing deeply into the blank white slate on the ceiling. Images came to her one by one—blowing out candles at their eighth birthday party, laughing hysterically at their failed attempt to stuff marshmallows in their mouths and say, "chubby bunny," Jade cannonball-jumping near her in the pool at Donte's fourteenth birthday party, the two snuggling on the couch after Jade's state championship loss. Pearl smiled at the visions as they came to her. Happy moments with her sister that would no longer occur. Nothing new to create, only moments to remember. Her breathing became labored as she felt herself sink into the bed, her body giving way to tiredness. Her eyelids blinked slower with each breath, fluttering on the way up as she lacked the energy to lift them fully. The intervals between her eyelids raising grew longer and longer until darkness finally took over. Pearl didn't want to fight it anymore. She closed her eyes and released herself, succumbing to her act as the rise and fall of her chest came to a halt.

No more pain.

……

Sander ran down Pearl's street as fast as his legs could carry him. He could see the Juarez house come into sight, which made him attempt to go even faster and nearly take out a child on her bike. Sander no longer possessed the capability of feeling Pearl's soul. He couldn't sense anything happening with her, though she was all he could think about. He made a hard-right turn and headed straight for the door and began banging. "Pearl!" he shouted. "Pearl! Open the door! Pearl!"

When nobody answered, Sander did the only thing he could think to do. His adrenaline took over as he stepped back and let out a loud grunt, kicking the door in and breaking it away from its frame. For a second, he shocked himself with what he'd just managed to do. Andrew, who was sitting on the couch with his headphones on blasting music from his phone, stared at

Sander in complete shock.

Sander ran past Andrew shouting "Call 9-1-1!" as he sprinted up the stairs. He could see Pearl lying in her bed, angelically motionless in the deepest sleep, which didn't settle right with him. He lifted Pearl's head and lightly shook it to wake her up, "Pearl. Wake up, baby, wake up." He felt for a pulse but couldn't find one. "Oh no!" he shouted as he began CPR. In between breaths, he half-shouted, half-panted, "Help her, please!" and "Come on, baby!"

"You're not supposed to see me this soon," he said, hoping she would suddenly wake up and agree with him. While desperately continuing breaths and compressions, he continued his one-way conversation with Pearl.

"Why would you do this?"

"This can't be happening."

"I shouldn't have left."

"I love you, Pearl. Please wake up."

"1,2,3,4,5,6,7,8,9,10,11,12,13,14,15," he counted, pumping her chest in hopes her heart would get the memo and start beating.

As Sander leaned down to breathe into Pearl's mouth between pumps, he wanted so badly to stay lip-locked with her. He wished more than anything that his energy could revive her, but he knew that would be impossible.

The paramedics finally arrived and took over as Sander watched helplessly from the corner of the room. Sander picked up his phone and dialed a number he dreaded calling, Marlene and Jeff.

"Sander?"

"There's been an accident."

"Accident? What happened? Did something happen with the kids?"

"Yes. It's Pearl. She's on the way to the hospital. How far away are you?"

"About three hours. Driving back right now."

"Okay, I'll have more details by then."

……

Marlene could barely believe what she'd just heard. "She did this deliberately, Jeff. I know it."

"Marlene, Pearl wouldn't do this on purpose."

"Jeff, she's been so depressed. We should have watched her better. How could we not have realized she was capable of doing something like this? How could we have taken off for the weekend knowing she has been struggling?"

"We could be the most supportive parents in the world, but if she is at a point where she sees this as her way out, then she will make it happen. I hope she failed; I really do. I want her to see there is more to life than this. She deserves more. A lot more."

Silence filled the car as Jeff choked up.

……

Sander sat anxiously in the hall, waiting to hear Pearl's prognosis. Dr. Patel emerged from the ICU, his look somber and regretful. Sander jumped up and hurried over to speak with the doctor. The nurse intercepted him and explained that, since he was not family, he could not see the patient unless the parents gave permission. Sander explained his role as boyfriend and confidant to the nurse, who reluctantly allowed him access to Pearl. Dr. Patel approached and gave Sander the update.

"She managed to put herself into a coma."

"Managed?"

"The pills mixed with alcohol should have killed her. We were able to get them out of her body, but there is damage. How long until her parents arrive?"

"A few hours," Sander said. He pulled out his phone and opened his messages.

SANDER: Going to be a while.

ADELAIDE: OK. How's it looking?

SANDER: Not good. Attempted suicide.

ADELAIDE: Oh no. I will keep Jade calm. Do what you need to do, and please keep me updated.

SANDER: WILL DO.

Sander returned to the waiting room to sit with Andrew, who was still absorbing what happened.

"Why did this have to happen?" Andrew asked.

"Sometimes, we don't know and never get to find out."

"Maybe this is the best for her."

"Don't. Not now."

"Jade and she were like this." Andrew overlapped his index and middle finger. "They did everything together. Maybe this was Pearl's attempt to join Jade. Would it be horrible to say it may be better for her? I mean, I would be comforting to know she is happy with my sister in some sort of beyond, rather than down here, miserable and crying because her heart is missing its biggest piece." Andrew paused. "Now I feel bad even thinking about it. Who sits there, thinking that the best thing for his sister is to die? What's wrong with me?"

"I don't think there is anything wrong with you. I've experienced this several times with families."

"What?"

"Never mind"

Andrew nodded. "Sometimes, you are so out there, bro."

The two sat in silence until Marlene and Jeff arrived. Andrew entertained himself with his music while Sander stayed busy thinking about his time with Pearl—both good and bad.

Marlene ran through the emergency room doors in a frantic state. Sander said nothing to her but only gestured in the direction of Pearl's room. Sander watched as Marlene and Jeff spoke with the doctor regarding Pearl's condition. Shock overcame Marlene at the information being relayed to her. On occasion, she released her hand, which was pressed to her mouth, to feel her chest.

Sander glanced at Andrew, who was still engulfed in his melodically infused fantasy. Sander nudged him on the arm. Andrew glanced over and removed his headphones.

"I have to leave. Please tell your parents I will be back soon, okay?"

"Will do."

Sander knew this needed to be family time. He experienced situations like this many times before and didn't want to experience it with the family of someone he deeply cared about.

Sander strolled through the hospital's front doors and down the dark boulevard until he came upon the ice cream shop he had taken Pearl to a few weeks prior. He walked inside and sat at their table, staring out the window, not noticing his trance-like state. When the server arrived at his table and asked if he wanted to order anything from the menu, Sander ordered a banana split and an Oreo supreme.

Absorbed in his thoughts, Sander sat and ate both his and Pearl's order on that lonesome evening—his own heart missing a piece.

TWENTY-ONE

"Can I come in?" Adelaide asked as she peeked her head through Jade's bedroom door. Jade said nothing. Adelaide made her way over to Jade's bed, where Jade had been lying for the past few days. Jade rolled over, her red cheeks and swollen eyes signaled her mood.

"I'm not going to ask how you're doing. I am going to ask if you need anything."

"Why can't you find out what's going on?"

Adelaide exhaled. "It's not a see-what-we-want kind of thing up here, darling. There's protocol we must follow. Dealing with the living is not within my realm. I am part of the transition team, so I don't deviate. I wish I could help; I truly do. But I can't."

"Why were you talking to Sander if he was from a different department?"

"Because he had the information I needed that related to your transition."

Jade stared at her intently. "Why didn't he know about Pearl's situation that… night? Being her Guardian Energy and all, I would think he could feel it or something."

"At the time, he wasn't assigned to her," Adelaide explained.

Pitiful excuse.

"Why? From what the amulet showed me, they looked like they were having fun. She seemed happy."

"It's more complicated than that."

How?

Jade took a second to think back to the images from the amulet and the fact Sander had not reported back to work in five days. Jade's eyes suddenly widened as she blurted out, "Oh, they fell in love, didn't they?"

Adelaide didn't respond, but her raised eyebrows and pursed lips confirmed Jade's statement.

I can't believe it.

"Wow."

"Jade?"

"Sorry. Can I be alone now?"

"But, you don't want to try to come to Group?"

"No. I don't want to see anyone right now. Please leave me alone." She knew her last visit to Group would indicate her final step before moving on.

I don't feel ready without knowing what happened to Pearl.

Adelaide didn't protest the request and stood up from the bed. As she proceeded out the door, she stopped and glanced back at Jade.

“You know, Jade, she would want you to be happy too.”

“That’s not a priority right now. I need to know what is happening to her. That will make me happy, calm, and ready. But right now, I’m not there, so please leave me alone.”

Adelaide exhaled in defeat as she proceeded to close the door behind her. “I’m here if you need anything. I will check back on you later.”

Adelaide’s parting words fell on deaf ears as Jade stared up at the blank gray ceiling, the final image from her amulet replaying in her mind like a broken record.

Ezekiel will have to wait for now. He will understand. Everything will have to wait.

TWENTY-TWO

What do I do now? I see and hear you, but I can't move or wake up.

Every day, Marlene and Jeff had come, along with other relatives, to pray for healing, and hope that Pearl would wake up soon.

Why does family only come around during dire situations? I haven't seen Aunt Beatrice in years. I feel so cold seeing Mom and Dad anguished. Even if I'm stuck, I feel no pain.

Sander had taken the night shift every night since Pearl was admitted. His time with her was more intimate at night, with less staff around and the hospital quieter than during the day. Each night, he held her hand, watched her charts, and contemplated what would happen if she did or didn't recover.

I like the warmth of his hands on mine.

Her condition hadn't changed much, and given Sander's profession, he knew the probability of her path more than her parents did.

As Sander sat beside Pearl's bed looking at her angelic face, he could no longer handle the lie he had told Pearl about himself. Though he could not take over her mind, he believed she could hear him. He leaned forward, took Pearl's left hand into his palms, and prepared for his delivery.

"Pearl. This is harder to say than I ever imagined. There's something I must tell you, my love. You see, I didn't appear in your life by chance. My presence was deliberate.

What?

"But it didn't work out the way I had planned. Not at all. I have done this job for more years than I can count, and I have never come across anyone who stole my heart the way you have. Pearl, I'm your Guardian Energy. The person sent to protect you from harm and keep you on a positive path."

Guardian Energy? I don't understand.

"The fact that we are here in this room tells me that I didn't do the job I was sent to do." He felt his palms moisten as he choked back tears. "Sitting here now with you, I realize that my emotions for you were the reason I did not complete my assignment. My feelings didn't allow me to take care of you the way you deserved, and, for that, I am very sorry. Distance from you feels like smoke in my lungs—I can't breathe. You are clean air for me. I am so sorry I failed you."

Oh, Sander. I wish I could tell you I love you. This isn't about you, though; it's about me.

Sander spent the remainder of the evening staring at Pearl as she lay still in bed. She looked at ease, as though her recent tragedy held no weight on her chest. Jeff and Marlene arrived for the morning shift, Jamie in tow. Sander felt a light touch on his shoulder. It was Marlene, relieving him of his duties for the day.

"She's very lucky to have you."

"No, she isn't, but thank you."

"Of course, she is. You have been there for her every step of the way, and we are truly grateful for you."

He politely accepted her words and gave her a smile.

"Thank you. Okay, let me say my goodbyes, and I'll be on my way."

He hovered above Pearl's head, staring at her every feature from her plump lips to her raven eyebrows and onyx hair. He placed his hand on her cheek, which looked more porcelain than flesh-toned, and caressed it with his thumb. He leaned in further until his nose touched hers and whispered, "You're beautiful," placing a long, slow kiss on her forehead. He stayed hovering near her temple as he continued whispering in her ear.

Why is he saying this to me? What am I supposed to do with these words?

Sander completed his monologue and backed away from

the bed. He gave Marlene a customary hug and shook hands with Jeff and Jamie, then proceeded out of the ICU. Striding down the third-floor hallway, he didn't know if Pearl would wake up. Whatever her path, he could only hope it would provide her with what she needed to heal.

An announcement came over the intercom, "Code blue in ICU." Doctors and nurses sped past Sander, some in a panic, others focused on the task ahead of them. Sander stopped for a second. His eyes concentrated on the checker-patterned runner rug that would lead him to the elevator. Contemplation filled his mind as he debated which direction to take. Forward to the elevator, or backward to the ICU. Time froze. As the hallway filled with blue flashes from the impending emergency, he reluctantly continued toward the elevator. He glanced back at the ICU, fighting the urge to retreat and take care of her, but continued walking forward. Twenty steps later, he stood in front of the elevator, waiting for the doors to open as he stared at the down arrow button. Down meant leaving his love behind. It meant eternity without her. As the doors opened, he glanced up. Speech escaped him as his eyes fixated on the space in the back of the elevator. He stepped into the elevator with his emotions at a standstill and pressed the "L" button. He glanced up to see his reflection on the wall and focused forward as his hand fell to his side, greeted with a gentle squeeze.

"You came."

"Yes, I did. I had to do this for me. It'll be fine, Sander. Don't worry."

"Why?"

"Not now."

"But…"

"No."

"I'm so sorry, Pearl."

"For what?"

"For failing you."

"Nobody failed anyone."

Pearl squeezed Sander's hand, his eyes misting.

"Are you ready, Pearl?"

"Ready as I'll ever be."

Pearl tilted her head and placed it on his shoulder, gripping her free hand around his bicep.

"Okay, my love, here we go."

TWENTY-THREE

There were three knocks on the door, but Jade ignored the sound. She had spent several days barricaded in her room, refusing to leave, consumed by the unknown prognosis of her sister's condition. Adelaide had made several attempts to coax Jade from her lair but to no avail. Jade needed to complete one last step of the program by attending her last Group session, but she had avoided it because of Pearl's unknown fate. The door was not knocked on again for the remainder of the morning.

In the late afternoon, Sander peeked in. Jade perked up on her bed when she saw his face.

"Sander, what are you doing here? How's Pearl? Is everything okay? You have to tell me."

"You know I can't discuss that with you, Jade, but I will tell you that she is no longer in the hospital."

"Is she okay?"

Sander nodded. "Yes, she's fine. My concern right now is you. What's stopping you from attending your final Group session?"

"Pearl. I can't handle the idea of not knowing what happened to her. For me, being told she's no longer in the hospital and is "fine" doesn't bring me any sort of closure. In fact, it makes it worse."

"Would it make anything better if I said she's doing okay now?"

"Probably," Jade said, absorbing Sander's words.

"Why don't you go to your last Group session and see if it helps. Talking to others might bring you a sense of comfort knowing that Pearl is okay, and then you can proceed with your healing."

Why does it seem like he's pushing me to go? We rarely spoke before, but now he is trying to push me to attend Group. So odd of him to be pushing me like this.

Her stare produced no words.

"Look, Jade, I'm trying to help here. You closed yourself off because you didn't know Pearl's state. Everyone else has tried pulling you out, and now it's my turn. You're running out of options here, and to be honest, you can only hold yourself up long enough before you end up right back at square one. Would

Ezekiel have wanted this for you?"

Jade glared at him.

"Ezekiel… how did you... Adelaide." Jade sounded disappointed. "This isn't about Ezekiel."

"Yes, I know it isn't. It's about you. From what I've been told, you've gone really far as of late, and you now have what you need to make the decision. Stay and regress or go and progress. It's up to you. Maybe I'll see you at Group."

"Why would you be at…"

"Because." Sander flared his hands out. He proceeded to the door and turned the knob to exit. She knew he had a point. She could either decide not to attend Group and be stuck, or to go, save the progress she has made, and finally move on.

"It hurt."

Sander paused. "What hurt?"

"When I remembered everything, I remembered *everything*."

Sander turned his head in Jade's direction, "Explain."

"Dying. It hurt. When my memory came back, it brought everything back. The pain. The frustration. The agony of seeing her helpless."

"Frustration? Interesting word choice. How do you mean?"

"It was all so dark, except for a glimpse of light. Like a

window but frosted so I could only see a shadow through it. Her voice hit my ears like I had earmuffs on. I knew she was yelling but couldn't make out what she was saying. I tried to yell, but my voice didn't make a sound. I wanted the burn to stop. It burned so bad in my throat and stomach. The pressure on my chest as she pressed over and over was unbearable. I knew she was trying. I could hear the panic in her voice. I just kept thinking, 'save me, Pearl, save me.' And just like that, it all stopped. That's when I found myself here with no recollection of what happened. I have worried about Pearl ever since it all came back to me, and I can't help but feel frustrated that I can't help her."

"Thank you for trusting me with this information, Jade. I'm sorry that weighed on you. It was very difficult for Pearl to deal with what happened as well, as you saw during your second visit."

Why do you need to pull that up? I feel bad enough already.

"She is better now. I hope that brings some peace to you, knowing this. With all that said, I highly recommend that you attend Group today. It will be good for you. More than you think it will."

Jade inhaled deeply.

"Fine. Knowing Pearl is okay now is the only reason I'm going—so I can save my progress and move on."

"Great. Have a wonderful session."

Jade replaced her white polo with a clean one, brushed her hair, and made her way down the hall like she had done many days before. But this time was different; it was her final walk.

She remembered standing in front of the very same door, staring at the "GROUP" sign, hesitant about going in. This time, Adelaide wasn't around to give her a push. She needed to do it on her own. Jade took a deep breath, and with a forceful exhale, pushed herself through the threshold to a familiar voice. She froze in her tracks. Speechless.

"At first, I didn't want to do it. I just wanted the pain to stop. The darkness needed to stop, and this plan made that happen. Once I started, I couldn't go back. I literally couldn't because I felt paralyzed and couldn't do anything. Andrew was downstairs, but I couldn't move to yell for him. Then Sander showed up. When I look back on it now, I think I could have handled the situation better. The pain went away for me, but I didn't feel good about what I did. I remember at the hospital, my family members were all very sad. But, one day, I heard mom tell dad, 'Maybe she will be okay. If she goes, she will be with Jade.' And Dad seemed to accept this. At first, I didn't get it at all."

Chase shook his head in agreement.

“Until the last night with Sander.”

Pearl noticed the group and Chase were no longer staring at her. They were looking at Jade, standing by the door in disbelief over the person sitting in front of her.

“Hi, Jade.”

“Why? How? Sander said you were out of the hospital.”

“He’s right. I am out of the hospital. I’m here.” Pearl smiled reluctantly.

Jade stumbled back as though Pearl’s words tripped her from behind. She made her way to the door and knocked it open with her elbow, her body following suit until she stood in the hallway. Adelaide met her in the hallway. The two stared at each other as rage built up in Jade’s eyes.

“How could you not tell me?”

“You needed to see for yourself. If I told you she was here, I feared you would plummet in your progress by taking fault, and I couldn’t have that.”

“But you lied to me.”

“Yes. I’m sorry.”

The door opened, and Pearl appeared. She stepped toward her sister to give her a hug. “This must have been terrible for you. Please don’t take fault. I am okay.”

“You’re not okay, Pearl. You’re dead.” Sarcasm laced her words.

"I'm not in pain. It's hard to explain. I've missed you." Pearl leaned in and hugged her sister.

How do I even process what is happening right now? It doesn't seem real, Pearl standing here, hugging me and apologizing for everything she went through.

Pearl didn't let Jade go even though Jade didn't hug her back. Knowing she would eventually have to surrender, Jade released the tension in her body and raised her arms, wrapping them around her sister. Her favorite gift delivered right to her, making her whole again.

This time, Jade didn't let go. She squeezed harder and harder as reality set in that Pearl was with her in person. Adelaide and Sander stepped away from the pair who stood there embracing each other, the end to an emotional journey for both. The two didn't want to let go but also knew they no longer had to.

"Hey, Jade, you okay?"

"I can't believe you are here. I'm shocked, but I think I will be okay."

"Okay. Why don't we go back inside and finish Group? How does that sound?"

Jade nodded. The two made their way back to the Group session and sat down next to each other. Jade spoke about her healing process and how the effect of having support from

Adelaide and Ezekiel made a difference. Pearl continued sharing her experience of her last days and how overbearing her grief was. She shared everything until her last night with Sander, then fell silent. When asked to continue, Pearl kept the memory to herself. Following group, Chase informed all the members that today would be Jade and Pearl's last day in Group. Jade seemed surprised that Pearl had moved along so quickly.

"Wow, Pearl, moving on already?"

"Before coming here, I had some time to come to terms with my actions and choices that would ultimately bring me here. The few sessions at Group solidified everything for me."

"It's... unbelievable."

"You seem surprised. Or sad. I can't really gauge."

"I'm happy, just a little surprised."

TWENTY-FOUR

"This spot was mine and Ezekiel's favorite," Jade said as they sat down on the bench in the garden.

"It's a lovely spot. Peaceful. Tell me about this Ezekiel character."

"He's tall. Comes from a big family. Gives amazing hugs."

"Ooooohhh," Pearl interrupted.

Jade slapped her on the arm with the back of her hand.

"Shut up. Anyway, there's something about Zeek that makes me feel safe. As if I could be myself, and it doesn't matter what anyone else feels about it. With him, it's like we're the only two people in the room. It's such a magical feeling. My cheeks warm at the idea of him. We've talked about how the circumstances of us meeting were not ideal, but if our individual situations had never happened, we would have never crossed paths. That's such an odd reality."

"Sometimes, the most unexpected things in life bring about the most surprising results. It's strange. It almost feels like it was my destiny to end up here. I can't believe I just said that. Does that sound crazy, Jade?"

"Yes, it does. Is it your destiny to leave people behind in shambles? To have family and friends sobbing and broken over the bad choices you've made?"

"Maybe. We can't control how others react or feel. Should our paths be determined by others?"

"I'm not sure we will be on the same page on this one, Pearl. Let's agree to disagree, yes?"

"Fair enough. I can't explain it with Sander. He, 'poof,' appeared in Group one day, out of nowhere. I had an instant pull toward him, and he seemed to know me so well. Once, he said your name, and I was confused how he knew it. Looking back, I know he said it because he actually knew about you."

"Interesting isn't it. We find the guys of our dreams after we die. I would have never imagined that in a million years."

"Correction. I found mine before I got here."

The two giggled.

"Since we are both ready, we can move on. See the wall?" Jade pointed to the large ivy wall in front of them.

Pearl nodded.

"We go right through there. I sat and watched Zeek go through it, and every day since I've imagined what it would be like and longed for the day I would be able to join him."

Pearl placed her hand on Jade's leg. "Sis. I have something I need to share with you."

"What's up Pearl?"

"It's about the wall. I won't be going through it."

"Oh. Are you staying here?"

"Not exactly."

"I'm not following. Where are you going?"

"Home."

"Come again?"

"I'm going back home. I didn't die. I'm still at the hospital. Sander presented a plan to bring me here and help you progress so you can move on. He promised it would be good for both of us. I will admit that, on my end, he was right. I feel much better seeing you. Seeing you okay and talking about this man-candy of yours."

"Wait, so what happens now?"

"I go back home and wake up. Life starts new for me. I'm ready to be okay and heal. You will be in my memory, but this place won't."

"What made you decide to go along with this plan?"

"For five days—no, wait—six, in a coma, the entire time, I could hear what people were saying. Of course, there were the family members talking about the tragedy of it all, seeing as you had died months earlier. Aunt Maribel had the nerve to lecture Mom and Dad about their parenting. Mom and Dad were distraught for the first few days, like super distraught. Dad cried a lot, and Jamie couldn't calm Mom down."

"Whoa, that's major."

"I know, right? Then, one day, they are sitting there, and Mom comes off with, 'Maybe she should go,' which just pissed Dad off since he didn't want to see me leave. They tussled back and forth for a while until Mom said, 'You know, Jeff, she would be with Jade.' Dad stopped in his tracks and said nothing. He eventually seemed to come around to what Mom had suggested. Seeing our parents come to the agreement that I would be better off dead seemed strange. But in a sense, I understood where they were coming from. I was in real bad shape."

"Oh, I know. I was there during that one Group session. I also saw you through the amulet the night you went to the hospital."

"Sander filled me in on the amulet. It's another reason I decided to go along with this plan." Pearl smiled. "Mom and Dad showed up for the morning shift—that's what they called it—and, before Sander left, he leaned in and gave me a kiss. A firecracker went off through my whole body. Then he leaned closer to my ear and told me his plan." Pearl paused, her eyes wandered to the floor as she fidgeted with her fingers. "Then, he left. I didn't see where he went, I just knew that I needed to continue and do this for me. So, I left down the hall to the elevator."

"You risked a tremendous amount to do this for me. I love you so much."

"Does this mean you are good? Ready to go? Happy with what's next?"

"Yes. I definitely am. But only if you promise to go home and do everything you said you would. Stay strong. You got this."

Jade placed her hand on Pearl's shoulder, looked at her watch, and smiled.

"Hey, Pearl, it's 11:11. Make a wish. No telling, Okay?"

Pearl paused for a second. "My wish is about you. It needs to be shared. I get a free pass on this one."

"Hmmm Okay, sis. What's your wish?"

"My wish is for you to be happy. I wish for you to find everything you ever wanted the second you step through that wall. My wish is for you and Ezekiel to have a love that lasts for the rest of eternity. My wish is for you to love and be loved."

"I love you, sis. I hope he is still there when I arrive.

I'm sure he will be, I have this feeling in my heart. My wish for you is strength. Strength to go be the badass you have been your whole life. Strength to overcome this and represent us the best way you know how. I'm proud to be your sister. Always have been, always will be."

"Your words give me so much strength. I know Ezekiel will be there when you arrive. And I can't wait to get started when I get home. I think I can make a real impact on those struggling with the same things I've gone through."

Jade glanced over at the increasing illumination coming from the wall. "Looks like that's my cue. I'm glad to see you happy. You deserve it after everything you've been through."

Jade lunged over and embraced Pearl.

"Catch you on the flip side, sis," Pearl whispered in Jade's ear, a tear escaping her eye.

Jade stood up, her hand still clasped with Pearl's as she stepped forward. She took a deep breath, encouraging herself to continue her momentum forward.

You can do this, Jade. This is what you've been waiting for. Left step, right step, left step, right step.

Pearl watched as the distance between them expanded. "She's going to be okay," Pearl said as Sander appeared and hugged her shoulder. "She's going to be okay."

"Yes, she will. He's waiting for her."

"How can you be sure?"

"I know, my love."

Pearl placed her hand over Sander's as they watched Jade approach the wall.

Jade looked back at her sister, who smiled and blew her a kiss. She then gave Sander a quick nod of appreciation and disappeared into the ivy.

Pearl released a strong exhale and smiled, her focus now on Sander. "Shall we go for a stroll, darling?" she said, standing up to face him, her eyes full of happiness for her sister and excitement about her own life.

"But of course, my love," Sander said, guiding Pearl around the bench until they were standing face to face, hands clutched. The two strolled down the path of flowers taking in the sun and breeze as Sander placed unexpected kisses on Pear's temple; Pearl reciprocating the gesture with a squeeze around his torso.

……

Jade anticipated the light to be less bright. She continued forward into an unknown, blinded by the blank ambiance surrounding her. She walked through an abyss of white until she came upon an unusually solid but bumpy surface. As she continued walking, the ground became more recognizable. A cobblestone road appeared as the white mass faded to reveal a small street lined with little shops and cafés. Jade didn't know where she had journeyed to. People were strolling and talking. She began exploring the street, the occasional patron stopping to look at her for a second before smiling. The scent of roses filled the air as Jade strolled by a flower stand under the "FLORA'S FLORALS" sign. She stopped to take in the fragrance responsible for engulfing her senses between the rose cart and the local bakery shop displaying the most delicious tiramisu pastries.

"Boston," she told herself as she stared beyond the end of the road and the brick buildings connected to the harbor. She couldn't believe her eyes. As a child, her family would visit Irish relatives in Boston and Jade immediately took to the city. She loved everything from the history, to the buildings, to the unique local accents. It reminded her of her favorite movie about Boston gangsters. Boston had been her favorite city growing up, so this experience felt like a dream.

I wonder if I am ever going to run into Ezekiel. I can't believe he wasn't waiting for me when I arrived.

She didn't know what else to do but continue making her way around this new environment.

So, what's my next step?

She spent the latter part of the day exploring her new surroundings—the parks and shops. She spoke to some people who offered her a friendly hello, but nobody seemed to know where or what she needed to do upon her arrival.

Jade sat down on a bench near the harbor and watched through the buildings as the sun began to escape from the sky. She couldn't help but feel a bit let down, knowing that she finally made it here but now had nowhere to go. It all looked the same as it did in the living world—boats, water, people kayaking, shoppers, bike riders…

I feel much more grown-up now. What an incredible journey this has been for me.

Watching the scene transition, Jade felt comforted by the sunset. She sighed and smiled. She was relieved knowing that Pearl would be okay. She closed her eyes, taking in the sounds around her when she suddenly smelled a familiar scent from earlier in the day. The roses. Potent and beautiful. Jade opened her eyes to see one rose held steadily in front of her by a hand she knew all too well. An enormous grin grew on her face as she reached up and gripped the stem of the rose with her thumb and index finger. She moved it up to her nose, took a deep breath in, and lowered it to her lap, glancing up at the presenter.

"I knew you would make it here."

So did I.

……

The blue and white Victorian home stared back at Pearl as she stood in its presence, smiling, preparing to approach. She made the walk up the path, climbed the ten steps, proceeded up the path some more, and then took three more steps. She inhaled deeply before knocking on the front door.

Henry opened the door and stared nervously at Pearl. “Pearl?” he asked anxiously.

Pearl smiled. “Hey, Henry. I don’t suppose I can get our shoebox back from you, can I?”

Henry paused. Bewilderment slowly melted from his face, revealing a growing smile. “Sure thing, let me get it for you.” She could hear the sound of feet pounding on oak as Henry ran upstairs to retrieve the box. He arrived shortly after and handed Pearl the box, losing a large navy-blue button in the process.

“Damn, this box sure could use some updating. Care to come over and help me with this?”

“Really? I would love to. Thanks, Pearl. Let me just tell my mom. One second.”

As Pearl waited for Henry, she about-faced and took in the scene before her—kids riding bikes, the blue sky, the smell of roses. Pearl closed her eyes and absorbed the sun’s warmth as she smiled.

Life is beautiful.

“Ready! Henry shouted as he shut the door. Are you ready Pearl?”

Pearl glanced back at Henry.

"I most certainly am."

www.ingramcontent.com/pod-product-compliance
Lightning Source LLC
Chambersburg PA
CBHW071106100726
47908CB00008B/2283

9781734505061